Pterosaur!

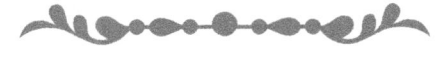

and Other Stories

NISABA MERRIEWEATHER

Pterosaur!
Copyright © 2024 by Nisaba Merrieweather

All rights reserved. No part of this publication may be reproduced, distributed, or transmitted in any form or by any means, including photocopying, recording, or other electronic or mechanical methods, without the prior written permission of the author, except in the case of brief quotations embodied in critical reviews and certain other non-commercial uses permitted by copyright law.

Tellwell Talent
www.tellwell.ca

ISBN
978-0-2288-4655-0 (Paperback)

TABLE OF CONTENTS

Acknowledgements v

The Next-Door Neighbour 1
Rumpelstiltskin 6
Stroke 16
Agnes the Hippopotamus 24
The Tarot Reader's Story 28
The Tale of the Snails 35
The Prison Guard 39
Interview with the Enbalmer 44
Pestering the Witch 47
Snail the Dog 50
The Wedding 57
The Pagan Speaks 61
A Love Affair and a Flight 69
The Horizon 74
The Soldier's Story 82
Biography of a House 87
Sixteen 91
The Weather Gods 96
The Goose Girl 102
Coming Out 105
Spiders I Have Known 115
The Disposal Unit's Story 120
Bluebeard 126
There Be Dragons 132
Gods' Night Out 134
The Cat Lover 137
A Disgrace of Angels 140

The Haircut	144
Love Letter to London	150
The Silk Road	152
This is not a Ghost Story	155
Watching Tv	158
Pterosaur!	160
Eater of Hearts	165

ACKNOWLEDGEMENTS

"The Soldier's Story" was inspired by a handyman called Luc who chatted about his traumatic past as he worked in my house. The use of mace was entirely factual.

I read "Sixteen," by far the oldest story in the collection, during open mic at Writers in the Park, a weekly event at Harold Park Hotel during the 1980s, when I was still silly enough to live in Sydney. The New Zealand author Patricia Grace was the invited speaker that night, and she loved it so much that after I performed it she moved tables to sit with me and chat for the rest of the evening.

"The Next Door Neighbour" and "Snail the Dog" were both performed at Originals Only Afternoons in Dubbo, run by the Outback Writers' Centre.

"Love Letter to London" was written for an online writing competition. It didn't place, but I'm proud of it anyway.

"A Love Affair and a Flight" was adapted from an anecdote told to me many years ago by an older friend, Edda Filson, before she died. She was tertiary-educated, but archaeology was my thing, not hers. She was an analytical chemist.

Most of the rest of the stories have been presented at meetings of the Outback Writers' Centre. And I thank them for their unfailing support since I moved to Dubbo, for their fabulous annual literary festival with all its beneficial workshops, and for the courage to define myself, finally, as a writer after all these years.

THE NEXT-DOOR NEIGHBOUR

At first I made friends with her, but that was a mistake. She was single and pregnant, which was immoral enough without giving the baby away, which she did, making it worse. At first I felt sorry for her and I opened my heart and my home to her, but as time wore on I realised she was talking as much to my husband as she was to me when she visited us, and I got worried. The crunch came when my husband said to me one day that she was a nice girl.

I don't know whether anything was already happening then, but I nipped it in the bud if it was. From that day onwards I refused to talk to her, or to even acknowledge her. If we met in the car park and she said "Hi Carolyn, how are you," I pretended I hadn't seen her or heard her. Eventually she got the message and stopped trying to talk to me. It was a shame, because she had become my best friend.

The balcony of her flat and mine backed onto each other. So one day soon after that, I threw away my husband's favourite potted rose bush, and told him that it had vanished off the balcony when I knew she was home. That way it didn't seem strange to him that I had stopped talking to her. After all, would he want his wife talking to a thief?

For months I watched her, determined to catch her out in some form of immoral act. Finally I had my chance. She used to be visited fairly regularly by a young family, a blond man, handsome in a common sort of way, his dark, small, beautiful wife (small, beautiful women are generally nasty, I find, so I don't tend to envy them their looks) and a couple of toddlers. When they first started, visiting the youngest was a tiny baby.

It was at the same time, or maybe a little later, that I noticed he used to come alone, too, in the middle of the day when decent men should be at work. He used to wear a uniform, proving he was cheating on the boss' time and cheating on the wife too. Why else would a man visit a single woman in the middle of the day when he is supposed to be working?

I considered it my duty to inform every wife in the building. After all, one day she might be after their husbands, too. I told them, just be careful of that woman, and don't let your man talk to her. I was quite disappointed that the other people around her still seemed to say hello to her, and the people she sometimes visited still let her into their flats. No matter—they'd been warned, so they were probably being more careful around her now.

Then came the night of the car burglary. Greg, my husband, had a habit of checking on our car regularly during the evening, just walking out the front and looking down at it to make sure it was all right. If anything woke him during the night he would get up and check on it then, too. And it's a very good thing he did.

Because one night there were a number of hoodlums trying to break into one of the other cars in the parking lot. Of course Greg raised the roof, bellowing at them and running after them when they took off. Lights came on in a few flats, including hers. I went outside to see what was happening and she was standing there, as cool as you please, with a totally different man dressed only in undies. He was grossly fat and really ugly. He went downstairs to help look for them, but by the time they got organised the car thieves had left long ago.

This fat, ugly man gave Greg a business card and said that his precious darling had been scared by some of the things that happened in the building, and he wanted Greg to ring him if anything happened. That's a laugh! We kept the card, just in case we ever found out the other guy's name so that we could tell him what was going on when we had some evidence. The fat guy is a high up executive in some posh computer company. He'd want to be—his only charm for her is probably his money.

They sounded like asthmatic whales when they humped, too.

Nothing happened for a while. She still had her daytime visitor and she still went off at night, probably to screw this other fellow. Then there was a long time when I didn't have anything on her, because her daytime screw didn't turn up and no one visited her at night. She took to leaving home for short periods during the night at different times and I could think of only one logical reason: prostitution.

Something had to be done to protect the neighbourhood, and I did it. Without telling anyone I bought a can of black paint at the hardware shop and a fair-sized brush, and hid them where my husband wouldn't find them. When he was snoring I got up in the middle of the night, turned the light on in the bathroom and turned a tap on slightly so that if he woke up he would hear a trickle, and snuck outside. This was my big chance. I wrote in huge letters all over her door "SLUT WHORE CUNT," covering the whole door with the words. It looked good. She would never think it was me, she would think it was one of her clients. And everyone else that lived in the building would see just how much trouble she brought to the place.

We are a quiet building in a quiet neighbourhood, and we don't want trouble. When Greg and I came home the next day he looked at the writing. He had no way of knowing it was me. "There are some sick bastards around," he said. I told him to calm down, there wouldn't be any more trouble. By the time the management had repainted the door a day later, absolutely everyone had seen it.

I was satisfied.

This was the time to complain to the management about her. Now that everyone had seen that, they would know that she just brought trouble and nothing but trouble to the building. Greg is allergic, so I told him her cats always play on our balcony. Of course, as soon as I told him that he broke out in hives, and then every time he went on the balcony he broke out in hives. Then I reminded him of the stolen roses. Then I told him that because he had a stuffed nose from allergies he couldn't smell anything, but the litter tray that she kept on her balcony was putrid. It turned my stomach, I said. Then I told him that the cats sometimes got out and sat on the car, leaving tiny scratches on the waxed surface above the paint.

That made him really wild, even though the scratches were left by a cat from downstairs, whose owner was nice and I didn't want to complain about.

Next time Greg paid the rent, he told the caretaker about all the trouble she had caused, she and her cats. He never got back to us. A few nights later I got sick and puked, and I told Greg that it was the smell of the litter tray that had made me puke. He believed me, because he couldn't smell for himself, and he got wild and banged on her door and started yelling at her.

She was too clever. She didn't start yelling back or swearing or anything. She even said the landlord's son had inspected the place because of our complaint and hadn't smelt anything. I think that was a lie because he never said anything to us, but I couldn't be sure. I didn't want to keep talking about that because she might say something that would make Greg wonder if there really was a smell, so I got him onto the hygiene aspect of it and onto the filthy noise the female cat makes whenever she comes on heat.

I wanted him angry, but he got too angry and started swearing. All this time she hadn't raised her voice and hadn't sworn, and I knew Greg was making a fool of himself. "Come on, darling," I told him, "don't lower yourself to her level." He stopped swearing at that, but didn't stop shouting. He threatened her with a health inspection, and was flabbergasted when she welcomed it, saying she had nothing to hide from him or the council. He suspected something was wrong, so he then said he was too busy to organise it. So she said she'd organise it, and he got angry again, telling her she'd only clean the place up spick and span before the inspector came if she organised it herself.

He came home, still shouting, then. I felt as if we hadn't really won that round, but I wasn't sure why we had lost it. All I know is that there were too many neighbours listening through windows to Greg making a fool of himself.

Some time during the next day while we were both out, she put up a trellis between her balcony and ours, and put a note under the door saying that it was to stop her cats getting on our balcony and bothering us.

I went out onto the balcony to measure where she had put the trellis, to make sure that she hadn't taken even one millimetre more than half the ledge that separated the balconies. I was absolutely livid to find that she had put the trellis wholly on her side, giving us the entire ledge. This meant I couldn't complain to the management, because I had suggested a trellis to Greg, knowing he'd never get around to doing anything about it.

Greg, the good-natured dope that he is, took that as a gesture of peace, and insisted I come with him when he went over to make peace. I had to hide my anger even from Greg, as well as her, and I even had to shake hands with the bitch.

The next night I thought I had her again. We got home, and a few minutes after we opened the back door onto the balcony she started playing a recording of that canned laughter they use for TV, really loudly. I knew it was her way of telling us she was laughing at us. I comforted myself by thinking that at one minute past the appropriate time I would be able to ring the police and complain about the noise.

Then one of the other neighbours visited her, a girl I knew liked her and hated me. I went onto the balcony to listen to their conversation. I couldn't hear anything, because they were whispering and giggling, but that told me enough. They were talking about me.

I kept watching the clock, and hoping she would keep playing that tape over and over. She did play it over and over, but at five minutes before the hour her flat went silent. Then I thought I could catch a whiff of something burning. Then I realised it wasn't just burning, it had a fragrance to it. She was smoking dope! We could get her on this one.

I told my husband about it, and like a dutiful citizen he rang the police anonymously, giving them her full name and address. We sat and waited. Some time later there was a knock on her door. We waited for the climax. Later we could hear the sounds of people leaving, so we went to the front window to watch her being escorted out by the police. They left without her. We still had our balcony door open, and a few minutes later I heard her go out onto hers, humming softly and apparently happily to herself.

I went out onto ours, on the pretext of shutting the door up for the night. "Oh hello," I said to her, pretending surprise and trying to sound pleased to see her. "You're out here, are you?" I didn't quite dare tell her it was way past any normal bedtime.

"Yes, I am," she said, sounding light-hearted. "I think the evening air is particularly good for you, and I just love the smell of incense, don't you?"

RUMPELSTILTSKIN

I believe in happy endings, even though I've seen few enough of them in life. And where else can you find happy endings reliably and often, but in fairy tales? Sometimes it is valuable to see fairy tales from the perspective of a character whose feelings aren't usually considered. Let's think about Rumpelstiltskin, for example.

Once upon a time, before the era of political correctness, lived a guy called Rumpelstiltskin. He'd had the misfortune to be born of short stature, and with a twisted leg, not great when your father is the village woodcutter–there was no chance he'd be able to take over his father's business. When he was a baby, his mother was advised to expose him in the forest so that he would die of cold or be eaten by wolves–it would be kinder than letting him suffer through a long life, the villagers said, patting her arm sympathetically.

But even though he was a twisted little thing, he met her eyes, and cried lustily for milk, and seemed to want to live and want human contact, and his mother was in the grip of her postpartum hormones, so against all the sensible advice of the villagers, she allowed him to live and even tried to raise him with love and acceptance.

At the village school he was bullied for his height and how he looked, for the weakness in his arm which meant he couldn't play cricket, and eventually he was even bullied for just being a long-term victim of bullying. From the time he started school to the time he left school, his life was a living river of misery.

When he came of age, his mother gave him a few silver coins tied into a knotted cloth, and told him to use them only in an emergency. Thanking her, he kissed her cheek and shook his father's hand, and walked down the path leading out of the village to seek his fortune.

A few years later the miller's wife in his home village died, and the miller married a much younger woman. Very soon she was pregnant, and gave birth to a beautiful baby girl, with skin softer than silk and a ready smile. The miller invited everyone in the village to the christening … and the village witch turned up, the one person who hadn't been invited.

Everyone had gifts for the new baby. The potter gave her a cup and bowl, the weaver gave her several yards of linen to make warm clothes with later, as she got older. Everyone gave her something, even the poorest. They might only have been able to afford a single apple or some brightly coloured flowers for her, but they all had something.

The Village Witch had nothing. "My gift," she said, "is my blessing and my curse. As my blessing, I give her the ability to charm everyone she comes in contact with. As my curse, she must keep every promise she makes, or ruin the lives of the innocent if she doesn't."

The little girl grew up, and both as a child and as a young woman, she charmed everyone around her. But she avoided promising anything to anyone, no matter how easy it seemed to keep those unmade promises. The words of the Village Witch, repeated often by her parents, hung heavy in her heart.

On his travels, it came to pass that Rumpelstiltskin journeyed past a vast lagoon, with a muddy mangrove forest at its edge. It was a hot day, so he took his socks and shoes off, and started walking through the cooling mud. Alas, he came upon a patch of quicksand, and found himself stuck fast and slowly sinking. He looked around desperately. "Help! Help," he called.

After a few moments of this, and when he was thigh-deep and expected he was doomed, he heard the welcome putt-putt of an outboard engine, and saw a tinny come into view. The tinny was being driven by a heavy, hirsute man wearing stubbies and a blue singlet, with a cigarette hanging out of his mouth.

"Hi there," he called to Rumpelstiltskin. "You seem to be in a bit of trouble. Do you need help getting out?"

"Yes, yes, please!"

"Just hold your horses, mate. There's one or two things we need to get straight first. Firstly, I am the Mangrove Fairy. A part of my brief is that I cannot rescue anyone who doesn't believe in fairies. Do you believe in fairies?"

If it was going to get him out of the quicksand yes he believed in fairies, and he said so.

"And we need to pay off the Quicksand Fairy, otherwise he will hunt you down wherever you are and steal your soul. Do you have something to pay him off with?"

Rumpelstiltskin thought of the twist of dirty cloth with its silver coins, that his mother had given him all those years ago, so be used only for emergencies. This was an emergency. "Yes I can pay him," he said.

The Mangrove Fairy seemed satisfied. "Right-ee-oh then! We're in business!" He pulled his tinny as close as he could, collected a coil of rope from the back of the boat, tied one end around his own waist, then threw the other end to Rumpelstiltskin. Rumpelstiltskin tied it around himself, too, and held it tightly with both hands as the Mangrove Fairy slowly started pulling him out of the mud. It took time, but eventually he was free of the grip of the quicksand, and with a bit of help hauled his muddy body into the boat. He lay there, exhausted, for a moment.

"Don't forget to pay him," growled the Mangrove Fairy, a threatening note in his voice. Whatever you have to pay him with, just toss it into the quicksand ripples where you just were."

Rumpelstiltskin pulled the bundle out of the bottom of his pocket. It looked really tatty. The Mangrove Fairy looked at him with deep suspicion. Rumpelstiltskin fiddled open the ancient knots and showed him the shiny silver coins, brighter than the day his mother tied them up. At a nod from the Mangrove Fairy he wrapped them up again, and tossed the small bundle into the quicksand. It disappeared slowly, leaving only a single bubble.

"Good," said the Mangrove Fairy.

"Thank you so much for saving my life," replied Rumpelstiltskin.

"That's okay. As the current Mangrove Fairy, it's a part of the job description."

"Nevertheless, I'd still like to thank you in some kind of tangible way. Is there anything you can think of that I can do now or even later to help you?"

The Mangrove Fairy hesitated. "Well, there is one thing …"

"What? I owe you. It can't be worse than drowning in quicksand."

"True. Well, it's like this, human. In this day-and-age it's hard, being a fairy. We live on belief, it's bread-and-butter to us. And it's incredibly hard finding sexual partners among people who don't believe, and who can't even see you. So, if you still want to thank me, I'd be much obliged if you drop your pants, bend over, and hold on …"

Rumpelstiltskin thought that was a fair exchange for his life, so he agreed, and it turned out he was right—being sodomised by the Mangrove Fairy wasn't as bad as dying. Later, the Mangrove Fairy fired up the boat's outboard, and they puttered off to a jetty, where Rumpelstiltskin disembarked.

"Well, thanks again," he said.

"No problem—thank you for the pleasure," said the Mangrove Fairy.

"Can you answer me one question before you go? I thought all fairies were girls."

"No, every fairy that's ever lived was a bloke. The Tooth Fairy, though—you really don't want to know about him. Oh! I nearly forgot! Because you were kind enough to believe in me, I owe you three wishes! What are they?"

"That I never drown in quicksand?"

The Mangrove Fairy snapped his fingers. "Done! But it was a silly wish. Think carefully. What else? You only have two wishes now."

"That I'm always in good health?"

The Mangrove Fairy snapped his fingers again. "Done. And your third?"

Rumpelstiltskin racked his brains. "Can I save one till later?"

"Nope. If we lose sight of each other, your unwished wishes are forfeited. I'm a fairy, not a bloody genie."

"Okay. How about I make one wish now, to be able to perform two miracles later in life?"

The Mangrove Fairy snapped his fingers. "Done," he said. "You'll need to snap your fingers and use the magic words. The magic words are obviously 'hocus pocus, here we gocus.' Think you can remember that?"

"I think so. And again, thanks for everything! It's all well worth a sore arse."

The Mangrove Fairy grinned mischievously, throttled up, and swung away. Then he turned and came back. "How old did you say you were, Rumpelstiltskin?"

"Thirty-two."

"And you *still* believe in fairies?" He laughed merrily, and left.

Rumpelstiltskin journeyed for many years, and saw many wondrous sights, but he never had cause to use up his miracles. In all that time, he never drowned in quicksand or developed serious health issues, so his faith in the Mangrove Fairy grew. The older he got, the more he wished he had a child. He had so much love to give, but was so alone in the world. And he would have loved to travel with a child, teaching that child everything he knew. He saw a lot of bad fathers over the years, and knew that the saddest child of his would always be happier than the happiest child of theirs.

Back in his home town, the miller's daughter grew up beautiful, charming and vivacious—the polar opposite of Rumpelstiltskin, in fact. She stayed single, though. From childhood she had been terrified of making promises, just in case circumstances would force her to break them, and she was very aware that the marriage service contained one huge promise. She had also watched people marry their ideal partners, only to dissolve into misery a few years later. She couldn't get divorced—that would break a promise. So she didn't marry.

The years dragged on, she got older. Her doctor mentioned in passing that she might want to crack on, get married and have a baby, as she wasn't getting any younger. And she started thinking of the men of her age in the village. She had known them all since childhood. Not many of them were single, except for those whose marriages had melted down into puddles of misery, and she didn't want them. There simply was no one to marry.

Then one day her father came to see her after a night on the turps, showing every sign of being delighted. "There's a rumour in town that a certain high-raking politician will be in town next week," he said, fizzing with excitement. "He'll be staying at the pub. Well—where else is there? He's about your age, he's single, he's rich, and he's looking for a wife. Best of all he's a politician, so he's away from home most of the time and you probably won't see enough of him to fight with him. Want me to line up a date with him?"

His daughter didn't think a politician would even listen to a lowly miller let alone date his daughter sight-unseen, but she assented doubtfully. Then she went to talk it over with her best friend. As luck would have it, her best friend lived next door to Rumpelstiltskin's ancient mother, and was the first person to notice when she didn't open her curtains. She called the paramedics, who took away the old lady's body.

"Someone should email her son," said the miller's daughter.

"Good idea," said her friend, and promptly sent an email. When Rumpelstiltskin received the email he was grief-struck, and immediately turned back to hike towards home for her funeral. He got back to town at around the same time as the politician and his entourage turned up. He stayed in his mother's house, which still smelled a bit of death even though they had opened all the windows. That night, he went to have dinner in the pub.

The miller recognised him immediately, and bought him a beer while he told the miller of some of his adventures. Eventually the politician and his entourage came into the bar, after checking into their rooms. Everyone knew immediately, because they were the only strangers in the place, and they were all wearing grey or midnight-blue suits with white shirts and solid-colour ties. Politician-clothes.

"Watch this," said the miller to Rumpelstiltskin, then walked over to them. He hailed the politician by name, shook his hand vigorously, and got himself introduced to the entourage, shaking their hands as well. He bought them a round. On that basis, they let him stay. Casually, he started chatting about his daughter, how she had never married because she was better than any of the blokes in town, how she admired him on TV, how she was cultured enough to converse with anyone but not rebellious enough to shame any future husband, and lastly, how she had admired the look of the politician on TV. Would the politician like to meet her?

He thought not. Women like that were a dime a dozen in his electorate. The miller had had a few too many–he raved about his daughter's lovely singing voice. Then her kindness. Then her healing hands. The politician still wasn't swayed. "What if I said," said the miller drunkenly, poking him in the chest, "that she could turn straws into gold overnight?"

The politician saw his chance. "Done! Tonight. I'll book another room here. I'll have straws in the room. By morning they must be gold or I'll have my boys kick shit out of you, understand?"

The miller staggered home gleefully to tell his daughter. Rumpelstiltskin, who had heard the whole exchange, practised his magic words under his breath. The politician went to the bar and booked another room, stealing one of the containers of straws from the bar as he left. Rumpelstiltskin sat there, biding his time and nursing his drink.

Later the miller returned, dragging his daughter by the wrist. He found out which room was hers, and dragged her there. Rumpelstiltskin followed at a safe distance. The miller went away. Inside the room, he could hear her sobbing. Of course the poor girl couldn't turn straws into gold. But perhaps Rumpelstiltskin could.

Gently, he tapped on her door.

"Go away!"

"I'm here to help you."

"You can't help me. Nobody can help me. My father really is an idiot!"

"Yes he is, but I think I can fix things for you. Let me in so we can talk about it?"

There was a long silence, then she unlocked the door and let him in. Her hair was messy and her face was blotchy and swollen. All the bottles in the minibar were already empty and scattered around. And on the coffee table was the container of straws from the bar, still stubbornly made of paper.

In the face of her despair it was time to level with her. "Look," he said. "Years ago, while I was travelling, I met up with the Mangrove Fairy. And I ... um ... did him a favour. He was so grateful that he gave me the ability to do miracles. I still have a miracle or two left over. Would you like me to miracle those straws into gold?"

"Um, yes."

"There's a catch."

She looked at him suspiciously. "What?"

"Well, I've wanted to be a father forever, but I just haven't found the right woman. I'm full of love. I'd make a great dad. You look healthy enough to just keep popping babies out—what if you were to give me your first one? You'd be able to visit as often as you liked, how about it?"

The miller's daughter sniffled a bit. That sounded suspiciously like a promise to her, but it just might be a promise she could keep, if it meant a future with a wealthy man. She agreed.

"Good," said Rumpelstiltskin. "I can miracle the straws on the spot. I'll need for you to stand in that corner with your eyes tightly shut, and your hands over your ears while I do my miracling." When she did as he said and he was satisfied she couldn't see or hear anything, he leaned over the container of drinking-straws and whispered "Hocus, pocus, here we gocus," then snapped his fingers.

At first he thought the Mangrove Fairy had conned him. But after a few seconds the straws shimmered, and turned yellow, then golden, then into heavy metallic gold straws. The container overbalanced with their weight, and they clattered noisily on the glass table.

She spun around. "Oh Rumpelstiltskin," she exclaimed, overjoyed. "How can I ever repay you?"

He smiled gently. "You can repay me by keeping your end of the bargain when the time comes."

"Deal," she said, and they shook hands solemnly. Rumpelstiltskin went back to his mother's place, and the girl slept deeply and dreamlessly. In the morning, the first thing she did was check the coffee table. Yes, it wasn't a dream–there were heavy gold straws scattered all over it, just where they fell.

After breakfast, the politician and two of his heavies came to her room. She opened the door a crack. "Are those straws gold yet?"

In reply, she flung the door all the way open. Their eyes were dazzled with the shine of morning light from the window reflecting on the gold straws. The politician gestured to one of his men. The man walked over, picked one up, examined it closely.

"Ya know, I think they're twenty-four carat," he said, surprised.

"Cool," said the politician, hiding his excitement. If he played this right, he could be rich beyond his wildest dreams. He turned to the girl and said "You're not out of the woods just yet. That was just a teaser. Today, you will spend the day in this room. You will see nobody, you will speak to nobody. Before sunset we will get every straw in this grubby little town into this room, and you will turn them into gold before breakfast tomorrow, understood?"

The girl nodded her head miserably. They went away. In the late afternoon one of them came back with a wheelie suitcase. He pulled out of it twenty-four dozen packets of straws, gave her a smile and left, locking the door after himself. She threw herself on the bed and cried. She couldn't do it without that hideous little man, and he wasn't around.

But after it got dark there was a tap on her door and there he was. She turned her eyes away and covered her ears. He leaned over the piles of packets of straws. He whispered "Hocus pocus, here we gocus," and snapped his fingers. The straws turned to gold. The weight of them was too much for the coffee table, and the glass tabletop cracked partway through.

"Be careful about that," he said, indicating the crack. "I'd hate for you to get hurt. Remember our deal–I'll see you when the time comes."

She gave the ugly little man a warm hug out of gratitude, then went to bed and slept soundly. In the morning the politician checked the straws, then proposed to her. She accepted. He didn't even mind the cost of the engagement ring–it was the tiniest fraction of the value of the gold straws, which he immediately sold.

They had their wedding, and all the paparazzi were there, snapping for the society pages. She charmed everyone. Then she moved to the city to live with her husband, leaving behind her father, best friend and Rumpelstiltskin. She thought about the first two occasionally, but never about the third.

Not until she was pregnant. Rumpelstiltskin didn't show at her wedding, so after a while she decided he had forgotten about her and their agreement. Not so. Even if he had, he would have been reminded by the gutter press, reporting on every aspect of her pregnancy. And come the day, her husband's sidekicks whisked her off to hospital and, after much heaving and groaning, the requisite son was born.

A son: a writhing tadpole, greyish and wet, smelling rather like the liquid on a freshly-laid egg. And Rumpelstiltskin did not materialise in her hospital room, so she was safe to keep him and love him. Her husband brought her home, and she started sleeping in the single bed next to the cradle in the nursery, because the politician needed his sleep so that he could be fresh for parliament and for the cameras.

After a few days, she was alone again with her baby, feeding him. She was sitting in the kitchen with the radio on reminding her that there really was a world out there, when there was a tap on the back screen door. She looked up–Rumpelstiltskin was there. "Come in," she called over her baby's head.

"Lovely boy," he grinned, looking down at the baby. "So beautiful. He's completely stolen my heart. You can keep feeding him, then say goodbye and we'll be off. Don't worry, I have all the supplies I could possibly need."

The young mother panicked. She couldn't possibly lose her son. She remembered the blessing and cursed placed on her as a baby—she was going to have to risk the curse. She simply couldn't lose the child!

"No," she said. "Go away. He's mine. You're not getting him."

This is the point at which regular tellings of the fairytale go on to have Rumpelstiltskin disappear in a puff of impotent rage, and she and the baby live happily ever after. But what of Rumpelstiltskin? It was no fault of his own that he was ugly and misshapen. It was no fault of his that he couldn't form a normal relationship in the normal way, and have a baby in the normal way.

And he was probably right, he might have made the most fantastic father! Almost anyone would have been a better father than the politician. But he couldn't, so all he could do was make an agreement, a moral and binding agreement with a woman who was prepared to let him adopt her child.

And she let him down. For that, generations of fairy-tale readers hated him and sided with her. It's the whole ablest narrative: if someone is disabled, deformed or even just ugly, they must of necessity be evil, no matter how good-hearted they are. Fairy tales are horrible. Humanity is horrible. Why couldn't she have had a little compassion, and honoured their agreement? Rumpelstiltskin suffered for the rest of his life, and lost the last shreds of trust in humanity, fulfilling the Fairy Godmother's curse.

But this is a fairy tale, not reality. So the ugly little man disappeared in a puff of impotent rage and everyone lived happily ever after, even though the girl couldn't magic straws into gold to make the politician rich beyond rich, and he might have felt swindled and made her life a misery because of that. Happily ever after. Certainly.

STROKE

Forty-seven is a prime number. And not any prime number, but the fifteenth prime. When I was forty-seven, my daughter was fifteen. It was an interesting age for me to be. Not young enough to be fresh and vigorous, not old enough to be completely worn out. Arguably, forty-seven is in that sweet spot when we are most ourselves: developed, but not yet in decay. Which is why it comes as a terrible shock to have a stroke at forty-seven.

As a teenager, my daughter loved roast pork. At any age, I didn't. So once a fortnight, sometimes once a week, we'd walk to the club half a kilometre from home, she'd have a big plate of roast pork, and I'd have a plate of something else. This particular night had to be winter, or at most the beginning of Spring or the end of Autumn, because the air was crisp and cutting on our skins as we walked.

Because I was with an under-age person I was never going to be unsociable and have alcohol with my meal, so we were both drinking orange juice. The table we had chosen was in the middle of the dining area, and there was a pillar behind her with a clock on it. Every so often I glanced up at the clock, because it was a school night.

She had made inroads into her pork, and was chatting away happily. I put down my cutlery, had a sip of my juice, and glanced up at the clock briefly. And got stuck. I couldn't drag my eyes away from the clockface at all. Experimenting, I couldn't move the hand that was resting on the table next to my plate, either, not even a single finger. She kept talking. I couldn't talk or move.

Then my hearing started to fade. Her voice got further and further away, until it and all the background-noise of a busy dining hall vanished down a dark vortex of silence. The feeling in my body started to fade, too.

Still looking at the clock, in my peripheral vision I could see my daughter stop talking and start to panic. She'd noticed something wasn't right. She pushed her chair back and came around to my side of the table.

By the time she got there and put her arm over my shoulders, I could barely feel it. She was talking and moving, but I couldn't hear or feel any of it.

Then my vision started to change. An ornate black lacy curtain came between me and the world. Deaf and without touch, I watched as the lace got thicker and thicker, until all there was left was blackness in front of my eyes.

This was perplexing. I couldn't move or communicate, couldn't feel or hear, and couldn't see. To someone else that would look like unconsciousness, but I was still very definitely conscious and thinking. I imagined what it would be like if this state was my new permanent reality. I couldn't see, hear, feel, react. But I was conscious and thinking! Very much so.

If this persisted, I'd have to be looked after. They'd put me in a hospital or nursing home bed. I'd be fed by tube. My arse would be wiped by carers. At first that sounded horrible, then suddenly not so bad. If I couldn't feel them tending me, why would I be bothered? And I'd be freed of any need to do anything: I wouldn't have to work, pay bills, or be polite to people I'd rather blow off. I could spend the rest of my life–years, decades–just in this comfortable dark silence, free just to think, something I loved doing anyway.

That seemed irresistibly tempting. Almost too good to be true. And like all too-good-to-be-true things, it ended. Just as I was getting completely reconciled to a future in that state, I started fading back in. Gradually the blackness turned into a thick black curtain, then into thick black lace, then thin lace, then something approximating normal vision. My eyes were still fixed on the clock.

When I had my vision back, the sense of my body started fading back in. Gradually, I felt the weight of my daughter's desperate arm across my shoulders. I tried to move my hand on the table–it twitched slightly. I tried to take my eyes from the clock and found myself looking at the woodgrain of the table and the detritus of our meal.

Then my hearing faded in. "Mum! Mum! Are you okay?" She wouldn't have been still saying that after a long time–all my thinking must have taken only a few seconds.

I tried to say "No, not really." It came out as an indistinct mumble.

Suddenly she snapped into being the adult. "Come on. We're going home."

I was so glad we hadn't driven! She couldn't drive yet, and I was pretty damn sure I wouldn't be safe on the road. I tried to stand up. I swayed a bit. I steadied myself. I started walking to the exit. When I say "walking" it was closer to an inchoate stagger.

And I was painfully aware of my gait. Here I was, coming out of a building that sold alcohol, staggering like a drunk while I'd been on orange juice all evening. Everyone would assume obscene levels of intoxication. There was no justice.

The stagger continued. Every time I had to step down off a kerb or up onto a kerb I tripped and stumbled, my daughter grabbing an arm to steady me. Instead of walking past a telegraph pole, I slapped right into it face-first, ending up bruised and full of splinters. Eventually she grabbed one of my arms and didn't let go, steering me home.

As we got to the house, she told me to open the door while she rang triple-zero. I obediently put my hand into my left-front jeans pocket, and pulled out my keyring on automatic. I looked at it in my hand as she talked to the operator. Somewhere in that tangle of metal things, a wooden thing and a leather thing was the Secret to Opening the Door, I knew that. I had used that tangle of nonsensical objects to open the door countless times. I looked at it helplessly, unable to access that secret, unable to even choose the thing that would open the door.

She finished talking to the operator and, exasperated, grabbed the tangle out of my hand and opened the door. Simply. Quickly. I was full of admiration for her competence. The house was dark and cold. She turned on a light. She made me lie down on the lounge, and every time I tried to sit up to reclaim a little dignity she made me lie down again, because that was what they told her. She said I wasn't allowed to have anything to eat or drink–the horse had already bolted on that one. But knowing I wasn't allowed, I was suddenly terribly thirsty. She was harsh, and didn't allow me even a sip of water.

We heard the sirens at a distance. They cut out, and it was silent flashing lights that pulled up in our drive. She let in the paramedics. I remember they were kind, and put a heart monitor on me. Cold, sticky tabs on my bare skin on a freezing evening. I protested. One of them told me my daughter had said I was having a heart attack. I tried to say I was pretty sure it wasn't my heart, I was pretty sure something had happened inside my head. The words came out wrong.

My daughter said something to them about my younger brother having had a heart attack. After a time, one of them told me my heart rhythm was healthy, but they'd take me to hospital anyway for overnight observation hooked up to a more sensitive cardiac monitor. Again, I tried to say that I didn't think anything was wrong with my heart, I was more worried about my brain. Again, they didn't understand me.

Very gently, they removed their portable monitor, brought in a gurney, and lifted me onto it. Wheeled me into the back of the van and clipped the gurney in securely. One of them went into the driver's seat, the other sat next to me. The last thing I saw through the back window was my daughter's face as she sat on our front doorstep. Devastated. I knew she'd get herself off to school in the morning. But in that moment, she looked heartbroken.

Because they decided I wasn't actually dying, they drove without siren or lights at normal road-speeds. The house was about equidistant to the two major hospitals in the area, and I knew they were both about twenty-five minutes' drive at legal speeds. Making an effort to speak clearly, I asked which one we were going to.

"Wyong."

That was good news. A friend of mine worked as an emergency nurse at Wyong. I told him that.

"What's her name?"

"Ambrosia."

"I don't know the name. What does she look like?"

Now, I *thought* I would have said something like: tall, very pale, slender, around my age, with long, curly red hair. That was, after all, how she looked. I said whatever I said.

"Yeah, I think I know her."

We pulled up at the hospital. They rolled me indoors where it was slightly warmer, if noisier. One of the paramedics waited with me, until he could do the handover to hospital staff.

"There's your friend!" He was delighted, and pointed.

He pointed to a short, dark, plump Maori or Pacific Islander, with shortish straight hair.

What on earth had I said? Obviously the brain-to-mouth link was still badly scrambled.

When the handover was done the lovely paramedic went away and hospital staff put me into a cubicle and hooked me up to a much larger and more intimidating cardiac monitor. More cold, sticky tabs on my bare skin. Nothing but a thin hospital gown against the air-conditioned but still cold night air. I said once again that I didn't think I'd had a heart attack, I thought something had happened inside my brain.

They smiled at me. I was wrong. My daughter had told the operator and the paramedics I was having a heart attack, so they were monitoring my heart overnight. If my heart's rhythm remained good all night, they'd give me a cup of tea in the morning and send me home. This was meant to be reassuring. It wasn't. I spent hours watching the numbers and symbols on the monitor's screen. I knew my heart was fine. I was worried about my brain.

Yes. My brain was worried about itself. I saw the irony.

The shifts changed at six and six. If Ambrosia wasn't working nights that week, she'd come in around dawn. The hours crawled. My heart kept beating regularly. The sky in the small, square window above me lightened to a paler shade of darkness. Morning-shift staff started turning up–I could just see the staff desk through my half-open curtain.

Ambrosia was one of them. As soon as she'd been through a rundown of her patients, she came directly to my cubicle. I sat up, she hugged me. Looked at the monitor and the notes. Unhooked me, stayed with me as I put on my now-grubby clothes.

"You're free to go," she said. "Have you got money for a cab?"

"I don't have my bag with me. They just took me."

"I'll ring my daughter and get her to drive you home. She knows where the house is."

It didn't take long for her daughter to arrive. She drove me home with minimal conversation, then took off as soon as I got out of the car. I panicked slightly. What if I couldn't work out how to open the door? I pulled the keyring out of my pocket. It made more sense than it did the previous evening. Now I at least knew what a key was. I tried all the keys, until I found the one that opened the door.

Inside, I realised my bladder was bursting, and I was starving. I went to the bathroom. The stream of hot, potent, early-morning urine didn't smell like hot, potent, early-morning urine. It smelled like charcoal-barbequed chicken. Every shade of wrong. I washed my hands.

On the kitchen table was the fruitbowl. In it were mandarins. Perfect. I grabbed the largest, and dug into the skin with my fingernails. The mandarin didn't smell of mandarin. It smelled of Mechanic's Workshop, the combined smell of ozone, hot metal, sump oil, dust, dirty rags and skilled tradesmen. Every shade of wrong. I didn't want to eat it, but I was very hungry. I broke off a segment and tentatively bit into it. It tasted like mandarin. I brought the remainder of the segment to my nose. It smelled of Mechanic's Workshop.

Wow. So now urine smelled of delicious, greasy chicken, and mandarins smelled of getting my car serviced? How was I ever going to live with this? (Simple. Time answered that question: I haven't eaten charcoal chicken to this day because of the association with urine, and I hold my nose when eating fresh citrus.)

I knew I had a few hours before my daughter would come home from school. I probably should see my own doctor and let her know what had happened. I dug out the surgery number, and asked for an appointment. "Is it an emergency?" the receptionist asked, as she always did. I considered my options. I wanted to be seen quickly. But equally, it was obvious to me that I wasn't about to die, and that I was a lot more capable than I was the previous night. It wasn't an emergency. She gave me an appointment a fortnight away, the first available without emergency status.

I spent most of that fortnight coddling myself. For that fortnight and a lot longer, my thinking was hazy. I'd start having a thought, and it would disappear like a lizard in the undergrowth, or like the cool morning mist when the day warmed up. Was I never going to be able to think properly again?

During that time, at first my daughter was very solicitous. She checked on my welfare, she did all the cooking, she forgave me everything. But after ten days or so, she started calling me stupid when I couldn't function to my previous level. I felt humiliated. And, told I was stupid, I became even more stupid.

Over this period I was in a timeless state. I didn't notice the days ticking over. Memories that I knew belonged decades ago surfaced as if they were still happening. I couldn't write, and struggled to read. Time became a meaningless ocean drowning me, and smells, well, many smells were weird. They never went back to the way they were—with time, I just got used to them. Eventually I made my way to my doctor's rooms.

I told her I'd had my heart checked over during that night, but I was pretty sure it was my brain that had gone rogue, not my heart. She made me stand up and gave me some basic commands. I followed them. She said she thought I'd had a TIA, or minor stroke, and why hadn't I come to see her earlier. (Why? Because I wasn't dying, and you're always booked up!) While I sat there embarrassed and apologetic, she rang a neurologist. I saw the neurologist later that same afternoon.

Life became weird with the stroke, and remains weird to this day. I never have any idea whereabouts I am in time—I have to have ten or twelve alarms set in my phone every day just to make sure I get all the regular basic day-to-day self-care stuff done. Compared to the very organised and academic thinking I used to do, my thinking seems scattered, random and often chaotic to me, even though other people tell me I still present as intelligent.

Having a lowered level of thinking severely limits me, and having no grasp on time completely prevents me from living an ordinary life and doing ordinary things for a living. Can you imagine my trying to meet deadlines? Follow instructions to do things by lunchtime or by tomorrow? Just not possible. My sense of smell is still rewired, and probably will remain so until I die. I'm getting very used to urine that smells like hot chicken, so I never feel a desire to eat hot chicken because of reverse-association.

There are only two plusses in my state of new-normal. After years of staggering around not seeing dentists and not having seen a new doctor after however-many years in a new town, I found I can still write. Or perhaps, write again. In very short bouts. With lots of reading and re-reading of my own material. I still buy books, but reading them is difficult, and takes a lot of backtracking and re-reading also.

The second plus? I've had a musical/visual synaesthesia all my life—I still remember visions of the classical music my parents played when I was a pre-schooler. Synaesthesia was always a deepening and enriching thing to me, a precious thing. Until I went to school and got bullied for saying a particular piece of music was yellow, I had no idea it wasn't shared by everyone. From the moment the stroke happened, I had a different synaesthetic experience. Colour/music became colour/music/texture.

I also developed a separate taste/temperature synaesthesia, an unusual one, where vanilla ice cream might be cold enough for a brain-freeze but still tastes warm, and a meal involving certain ingredients straight off the stove will taste cold even as it's clinically burning my mouth. And the taste/temperature thing has, in certain taste-ranges, an undercurrent of textures, so sometimes it links up with music as well. There are some foods I know I can't eat when certain kinds of music are playing because they will clash and make me deeply uncomfortable.

For years after I had the stroke I felt that life wasn't worth living. I was acutely aware that I was functioning on a sub-par level. Slowly, that changed, I don't know when. I still get deeply depressed when I remember who I used to be, and when I try to think like her. But I've stopped looking so much at that, and instead I look at what I can still do. And I can still do some things.

I've had very close brushes with death three times in my life, so far. Now, I'm just happy if I wake up in the morning and I'm still breathing. I don't care that my body hurts. I don't care that my brain doesn't do its job. I'm breathing, and that beats the known alternative: not breathing.

AGNES THE HIPPOPOTAMUS

Agnes the Hippopotamus was sick of being grey. "Why, oh why am I grey?" she sighed. "Grey is such a dull colour. How beautiful I would be if I were not grey!"

Agnes looked at all the other hippopotamuses, her friends. They were all a boring grey, too, but they didn't seem to notice. The stupid, fat things were all lolling about in their wading pools or grazing on the foliage near their wading pools, or playing with their babies amongst the foliage near their wading pools. Not a single one seemed discontent with their boring grey skins.

Agnes was the only one. "Why don't you like being grey?" asked Charles, the oldest hippopotamus. "We have always been grey. You are a silly, frivolous fool. There is hardly time enough in life to enjoy the important things, like food and wading pools and babies, so forget what colour your skin is."

All the other hippopotamuses picked up their square, heavy heads and laughed at her, with that slow, deep laugh that only a hippopotamus can laugh. Agnes did not like being laughed at, any more than you do. With huge, salty tears rolling down her cheeks she left the wading pool and lumbered painfully across the drying expanses of the land.

On the hard, dry, stony earth the soft pads of her feet started aching, and before very long they were cracked and bleeding. The sun beat down harshly, hurting and drying out her skin. Agnes had never been so far away from a cool, wet wading pool in her life.

At long last she came to a grove of trees, and settled in the shade, utterly exhausted. A group of zebras ambled past. One of them noticed her and, curious, came over to talk to her.

"Venerable hippopotamus," the zebra greeted Agnes courteously, "you must be worn out. Why are you so far from home?

"I am so far from home," Agnes replied, "because I am sick of being grey and want to learn how to be another colour. Tell me, zebra, how did your people become striped?"

The zebra had never thought about it before. "I suppose," she said thoughtfully, "that it is because we run under trees all the time. Under the trees the sun and shade are bands of white and black on the ground, and they must have stained us."

"Goodbye then," said Agnes. "Goodbye, hippopotamus," said the zebra, and caught up with the rest of her herd.

Agnes got up and tried to run under the trees, but her feet hurt terribly and her throat was parched. She sank to the ground in despair. "I will never be striped," she thought sadly.

Just then a giraffe foal passed by. "Hello, giraffe," said Agnes. "Hello yourself," said the giraffe foal rudely. She was a very young giraffe, and her mother had not taught her manners yet.

"How did you get such lovely brown patches on your beautiful yellow coat?" asked Agnes.

The giraffe foal didn't know, but she pretended she did. "I eat the smallest, sweetest, juiciest leaves off the very tops of the tallest trees," she said. "My food makes me beautiful. You must eat really awful food to get so ugly and grey."

"Goodbye, giraffe," said Agnes sorrowfully. "Goodbye yourself," she replied rudely, because her mother had never taught her any manners. She wandered off to look for her Nan to ask why giraffes had their colours, and Agnes was all alone again.

Try as she might, the only leaves poor Agnes could reach were the old, dry, hard, bitter ones at the bottom of the tree. She was still grey after she ate all the leaves she could reach.

Next along came a lion. "Oh lion," called Agnes, really upset by now. "How can I get a golden coat like yours?"

"Well now," said the lion carefully. Lions try not to tell lies ever. "I suppose if you behave like me you might just possibly end up looking like me. All you have to do is sleep, wait around for lionesses to bring you everything they catch, eat the very best raw meat, leave them only the scraps, then sleep off your dinner whilst they go and hunt some more."

Raw meat! Agnes didn't like the idea -- she was used to a diet of watercress and daisies. (Your mother sometimes uses flower in her cooking, doesn't she?) She left the lion, knowing in her heart she could never be golden.

Sadly, she started making her way back to the wading pool. She was defeated and dejected. On the way home she met a brilliant silver and blue butterfly. The butterfly looked flustered.

"Oh hippopotamus," the butterfly said eagerly. "Tell me please, how can I turn grey? The savage rhino and the great big elephant wouldn't even talk to me, but everyone knows you are nicer."

Agnes was puzzled. Here was the most beautiful creature she had ever seen in her life, and it actually wanted to be drab and ugly! "You are so pretty," Agnes said, "so why do you want to be ugly?"

"I may be pretty," the butterfly began bitterly, "but I am also obvious. There are birds in the air and snakes in the trees that want to eat me, and my silver and blue wings make it easy for them to see me. If I was grey I could hide in the shadows or against the bark of trees, and no one would ever know I was there."

"I'm sorry, butterfly," said Agnes. "I never wanted to be grey, just as you never wanted to be bright. If you ask me, I think we were both fated to be stuck with the wrong colours."

"I don't know," replied the butterfly shyly. I think you are an especially lovely shade of grey." And before the astonished Agnes could reply, she flew off in a flurry of silver and blue wings.

On the long, dry walk back to her home Agnes thought a lot about that butterfly. She was certainly beautiful, but it was dangerous for her. And the butterfly really liked the idea of being grey.

At sunset, Agnes arrived home. She was tired and thirsty, and her dry feet hurt terribly. She plunged into the soothing, cool waters of the wading pool and drank deeply. Then she rolled around to get her back cool and wet.

"Why did the butterfly think grey was nice?" wondered Agnes. She craned her neck to look at her back. Not just grey, she realised, the water on her back reflected like silver. And all the colours of the sunset shone on her silver back, the pinks and oranges and yellows.

"The butterfly was right," said Agnes. "We only have to look at ourselves in a different way to see how beautiful we are."

THE TAROT READER'S STORY

An old man shuffled into a café. He ordered a coffee, then sat in a dark corner, in shadow, where he could watch the hustle-and-bustle of the workers and patrons, and where nobody might notice him. As he waited for his coffee, he pulled out a Tarot deck and started shuffling. Within moments someone noticed him. A woman wearing far too many rings walked up to him.

"Can you do me a reading?"

He thought she was rude and intrusive. "This is what I do for a living," he replied, as a gentle go-away-and-leave-me-alone.

"That's outrageous. If you were spiritual you wouldn't charge at all."

"You get what you pay for. In my case, you are paying for forty years of training and experience, direct contact with the divine, and bags full of raw natural talent. And spiritual people have a right to earn a living. Would you refuse to pay a doctor because they should have a vocation to heal and should be happy to do it for free and live on unemployment? Would you refuse to pay a pilot because they adored flying? Either you pay me or I don't read for you, lady."

"Oh." He thought she was going to back down and leave him alone for a moment, then she took a breath and met his eyes again. "Well, if you were any kind of reader, you could make that deck tell a story for our entertainment. I bet you can't!"

"I bet I can," he returned mildly. Quietly, he shuffled. Her voice was not quiet, and people had started watching.

When he was happy with the shuffle, he put the deck on the table. "Can you cut this in four piles, please? Just wherever it divides naturally, doesn't matter if the piles are uneven."

She did so. "Okay, now somebody else. Anybody?" A man in a reflective safety vest stepped up. "Now place the cards back into one pile, with a different one on top."

"Can't remember which one was on top."

"Perfect. Get them together into one pile any old way." The man did so.

"Okay," he said. "You two agree that the deck is now in whatever order you put it in between you? That I haven't arranged it in some way to make a story?"

They nodded. Everyone had gathered now, and there was a buzz of excitement.

"In a minute I'll turn cards, and make a story from the images that come up. The shuffling and cutting will have placed the cards in the right order. By the way, my name is Anxiety Jones. Blame my parents—I think they'd heard of Capability Brown, and wanted an equally weird name. It's been protective, though—I've never really had anxiety issues."

He turned the first card. It showed a pregnant woman in a flowing dress, trees behind her, stars above her, wheat sheaves at her feet. The card title said The Empress. Talking to himself now, he said "Someone who gardens, cooks, and has sex."

He turned another. A gold-embossed vision of hell was revealed. He grinned. "The Devil—secrets, darkness, and passionless, loveless sex. The Empress might be the Persephone to his Hades, so the dance of love and hate, and the change of the seasons. Just an idea at this stage."

He turned the third card. The Four of Wands. "Ah! The home environment. What would that be like, given the Devil's influence?"

Someone said "You haven't told a story yet. That's cheating."

The reader broke the spell that had cocooned him, and came back to the room. Glancing around, unsure who spoke, he replied "hang on a minute, I'm just turning cards. The story will start when I finish turning cards." He turned another card. "Ah! The Hierophant! Working in a major institution with traditions of its own, having names (all popes take on a papal name), keeping the wisdom of the past in the form of her ancestor's libraries. Now we're getting somewhere."

The next card, when turned, revealed Death. "Ah." He became thoughtful. "How can I, as a storyteller, make the listener think that someone has died, or even a few people have died, and another is a killer, while making sure no killing happens during the story?" He paused for a moment. "What do you think–do I tell a story from those five cards, or do I turn a sixth just to finish it off nicely?"

"A sixth," growled the woman with the rings. "And remember, this is a bet. As soon as you turn it over, tell us the bloody story."

He pulled the last card and placed it on the table above the row formed by the other five. The Two of Swords. An upright sword each side of the picture, a dark-haired woman with shafts of light coming out of her eyes. He couldn't help himself. He giggled slightly. "Yes," he said, "yes, I have the story. I'll let you all make up your own minds whether it's fiction, or a story from my own life. And no, I'll never tell, so don't ask."

I am in love with a terrifying woman. I ask no questions; I do not want to hear the answers.

She bakes her own bread, which smells gorgeous and which I do not trust, and grows her own vegetables, which look divine and which I do not eat. I fear that if I absorb food originating from her hands rather than from a supermarket, I may never cut myself free–the very cells of my body will be enchained to her, and they will die one by one, if I try to separate myself from her. That is a risk I cannot take, because one day when this spell is over or I am stronger than I am now, I will want my freedom. Never taste the pomegranate. Not one seed, no matter what form it takes.

I come to her house for sex. The sex is abrupt, savage, and totally lacking in foreplay. No sado-masochism is involved in any way, but I always feel punished. Afterwards, I lie there trembling in my own sweat, vulnerable in my own skin, watching as she smokes one and a half cigarettes, pinching off and throwing away the second half. It is the only time she ever smokes, and she smokes entirely without pleasure.

This is the Underworld, this is the darkness of dreams. Every time I come here something shifts behind the faded timber shutters; something shifts, and I always try to catch a glimpse of it. I never succeed.

I do not come to her house to eat. I have politely refused coffee, food, wine. We often sit on the front porch where the huge avocado tree casts afternoon shadows, indulging in uneasy banter about this refusal of mine. Once in the kitchen she dipped her fingertips in a small dish of a green paste which she said was garlic, chilli, lemon juice and avocado–a sensuous green paste that smelled like seduction. She licked and sucked her fingers with great deliberation, then dipped one little finger in up to the first joint quickly, and ran the silken green fingertip over my lower lip with a lightness of touch that took my breath away. Pungent and creamy, penetrating and sensual, it smelled like her.

I was almost undone. I almost licked my lips. I turned away, wiping my lip with the back of my hand.

Her house was a huge rambling bungalow; a bungalow in Bangalow, she used to quip. The flat metal roof rattled under the torrential rains and baked under the summer sun, the fibro walls supporting it refusing to release the heat it captured. In the living-room I could see where fibro panels of inner walls had replaced former windows and doors: the house was once far smaller. Now it sprawled over its quarter acre; every decade or so someone else had built another room onto it, boarded something up, knocked something down. Garden sheds had been attached to the back of the house with afterthought-corridors and afterthought-stairs, and had become guest bedrooms, and artist studios, and where she kept her exercise equipment. And those were just the ones I had caught glimpses of, through half-opened doors.

She never offered to show me around the house, and I never asked. I liked the mystery of it, liked being able to catch those glimpses occasionally, and look across rooms where other doors led into more mystery. The house had a dual identity: the original tiny box of its construction, then the extensions ranging away from the core of the house into mysteries I was never invited to see directly. She, too, had her own dual identity, calling herself Annie at the bank where she worked with her white skin, and Consuela at home where she watched me with her black, flashing eyes. Eyes like two swords, that would cut you as soon as look at you.

That mystery extended even into sex. She would meet my eyes with intensity, but I could never see into them. She would throw herself into sex with a savagery that was really too fast, raw and immediate for me, yet I always felt as if it was never about her pleasure and that she never lost control for an instant. Sex with her was horrible. I always longed to escape, then I always longed to return. Horrible.

And yet, she surrounded herself with things she couldn't control: half a dozen laying hens with a penchant for destroying things in a part of the garden behind the twists and turns of the extensions, hens that I sometimes heard but never ever saw, her parents', grandparents' and one great-grandmother's libraries packed into a "bedroom" the size of a small house and that threatened to engulf her as they had the previous generations, a violently insane galah which had to be battered into its aviary with a broomstick before it was safe to allow me into the house. All these things added their own violence and randomness into her world, a world I was permitted, unlike nearly all others, to glimpse from the edges.

One day, in one of her efforts to make me eat what I do not and cannot trust, she took me into the pounding sunlight of her vegetable patch. "Come," she had urged me, minutes before, with that helpless, concerned look that would be easy to mistake for something genuine. "I want you to see something."

There was a strip of threadbare lawn between these bits of the extensions, and beside it a rich, dark vegetable patch, the black, moist, fibrous soil significantly higher than the rest of the drier grey earth. I found myself looking at five mounds: five low rises of soil, their toes pointed towards the strip of lawn, their heads pointed towards the wall of the house. Dead bodies may have been lying mouldering under the rich, fertile humus—they were exactly the right size and shape for five shallow graves.

For a split-second, I saw my own future, and I nearly caught a glimpse of the thing that skittered through her bedroom when I was confused by sex. So it was here, too. I regained my self-control before my panic had had a chance to translate itself into flight, or even into facial expression. I couldn't say she never noticed—she has always been unreadable.

We walked to the furthest mound from the door, earth the colour of her Spanish hair and as damp as her tongue, covered thinly with shredded sugar-cane mulch. "This one," she said, pointing with her toe, "will have my asparagus coming up soon. They're already planted. I could harvest them immediately and have to replant, or I could let them go wild for a few years, and keep them as permanent plants for decades. This one," and she indicated the second mound, "is where I will plant my celery seedlings. I have seed in growth-trays in the potting shed which is starting to germinate. Celery needs to be mounded up."

Inwardly, I shivered, despite the heat of the sun burning me where the heated fabric of my shirt was brought into contact with my skin. She pointed to the third, the central grave-like mound. "See how the onion seedlings are lying flat?" I looked, and saw thin green lines, about as long as her stubby little fingers and very fine, lying flat to the ground, radiating out from what could be the spine of the mound. She saw me looking. "You plant them flat like that—you don't dig holes, not even tiny ones. Then you sprinkle soil over their roots, and mulch them. As they gain strength they'll stand up, all by themselves." Her voice was high and excited. "It's one of the miracles of nature."

She looked at the fourth mound, her face quite still for a moment. Then she moved away from it, and started talking rapidly about the tiny, dark-green, purple-veined leaves along the centre of the fifth mound, her beetroots. She baked beetroot like potatoes or pumpkin, she was telling me, or grated them fresh into salads or sandwiches along with their leaves which were nicer than the best lettuces and steamed up better than silverbeet or English spinach. She didn't like beetroot sliced and pickled like the stuff in tins, though every year she had too much to eat fresh without getting sick of them, so she'd always pickle some to give away to neighbours. Her voice continued talking but I stopped listening for a moment.

She even knew there was such a thing as neighbours?

In the heat, she seemed very far away. I hadn't caught up to her: I was frozen, rooted to the spot, beetroots or not, eyes locked down, unable to look away from the mound that she hadn't discussed.

"What do you fertilise with?" I heard my voice ask. It seemed unfamiliar in my own ears. She did a double-take, turned to face me and dragged herself away from her monologue to answer my question. "Protein-based things, mostly," she replied. "You know, fish emulsion, blood-and-bone, that kind of thing. If rodents or other pests die, I tend to dig them in, too."

Other pests. I was silent for a time, politely nodding and grunting assent at appropriate pauses in her running conversation. Later, as we went back inside, I asked quietly: "What exactly did happen to that ex of yours?"

"He is not a problem any more," she spat savagely. Her sudden vehemence startled me, and her eyes slashed the room, two very sharp and dangerous swords in the control (of a maniac?) "He will never be a problem to anyone ever again, if I have anything to do with it." She grabbed my wrist and jerked me into the half-light of her living room, where she flicked on the TV, its voices and music too sudden, too loud and too cheerful.

Like Persephone, I must never taste the pomegranate offered to me in the darkness of the Underworld. I must keep myself free. I must keep fasting to keep pure. I am in love with a terrifying woman, a woman with too many secret rooms, a woman with a glittering, dangerous smile.

THE TALE OF THE SNAILS

Judi was the youngest of four children. Her mother spaced them two years away from each other, and alternated the genders, so it went boy, girl, boy, girl. Judi was the youngest. I got to know her when she was in Sydney, where I lived at the time–I was introduced to her by her aunt, who hoped I'd be a good influence on her.

She was living in someone's garage at the time, sleeping on a bare single mattress on the floor that she'd picked up from a kerbside cleanup. It was a very ratty mattress. She had black, ingrained dirt under her broken fingernails. Her long and naturally frizzy hair had, after months or years of never being brushed, solidified into a single hard knot involving all of it, that banged against the back of her neck when she walked.

That sounds unprepossessing–but she had an infectious laugh, a generous-hearted intelligence and quick wit, and aside from her fingernails she seemed clean–she never had a smell to her. We hung out quite a lot–I was surprised to find how much I enjoyed her company. She was a bit of a lost soul, at least until she went to art school. When she finally went to art school her life improved out of sight, but our friendship started the long, slow crumble.

Before art school, she seemed to have no friends other than me. She told me a lot of stuff. Her father was a psychiatrist. And a complete loon. She never said anything, but I think he might have been a child-abuser as well–she was always on edge when she talked about him and I never met him–I met all the rest of the family. Her mother was a GP, who met her father when they were both studying medicine at Sydney University.

This would have been in the 1950s, and her mother, whom I met several times, told me hair-raising stories of discrimination at that time: of being called out to the front of the class and ordered to strip when discussing female anatomy, of tutors expecting sexual favours for good grades. And the autopsy. Yes, the autopsy.

She had to do an autopsy, with supervision by three teachers behind a window, as a part of the examination process. She was as nervous as all shit. A body was on the table, covered in a sheet. The three examiners were behind the window, giggling gleefully. She flicked the sheet off the body, to find, as she said, the biggest penis she had ever seen anywhere, and someone had written on it with a black marker pen "All For You."

What did she do? Well, what could she do? She wanted her grades. So she took a deep breath, tried to ignore their mirth, and made her first incision. What was I talking about? Oh, yes, the family structure. Judi's father was a psychiatrist. Her mother was a GP with a taste for small country town practices. After they divorced and the father remarried, her stepmother was an anaesthetist. Their birth mother was the doctor in the next town to here for about twelve years. Judi's elder brother, Barney, was called Rubble by everyone. Rubble was a gynaecologist. The next one down was Stephanie.

Honestly, if I had met Stephanie first, she would have been my best friend, and Judi would have been the sister of my best friend. But I met Judi first, so she was my best friend and Steffie was my best friend's sister. Steffie grew up with a mother, father and stepmother who were doctors. Her older brother studied medicine. When she did her HSC she got the required marks—she felt as if she had to do medicine.

She hated it. I kept in touch with her until she retired. She never, ever ran a practice of her own or bought a house. She'd locum or work as a registrar for eighteen months living in a shabby rental, then she'd resign, put her stuff in storage, and travel until the cash ran out. Then she'd get another job and find another house. Whenever she was in work, she was always really depressed. Whenever she was travelling, she'd be gone and I wouldn't see her until she was working again.

The third child was Matthew. Even as a foetus he was wild—their mother always said that if he'd been their first he would have been their last. As a child he got into fights at school, as a teenager he was stealing cars and speeding down the Great Ocean Road. Always a handful. But a very, very bright handful.

In his last year of high school, when he was on track to be dux, there were constant shouting-matches with his father, along the lines of Dad insisting that they were a medical family and if his grades were good enough he must do medicine, and Matthew saying he wouldn't ever, no matter what. It ended in punch-ups fairly often, with Matthew always swinging the first punch.

When he got his HSC he still insisted he wasn't going to do medicine, he wanted to be a leatherworker. His father said if he didn't do medicine he had ten minutes to get out of the house. Matthew packed a bag and ended up at his mother's door. No, she said, if you stay here he will kill me, but I tell you what.

And she bought him a campervan to live in. And a full set of leatherworking tools. And quite a lot of different kinds of leather. Matthew spent decades making stuff during the week, then going to local markets to sell it on the weekend. Occasionally he'd drive to a new town. His mission in life was making stupid women pregnant, he said, to increase the smart-genes in the gene-pool by preventing that pregnancy from being fathered by an idiot. He had around thirty children, last I knew.

Judi had watched this carefully. She also wasn't going to do medicine. So when the time came, she quietly packed her bags and slept at her aunt's place until her father made a scene, then was homeless for a while until she found the garage where she was living when I met her. She picked up a bit of work as a kitchenhand and lived in shared households for most of the years we were friendly.

Then after a decade or so she went to art school. She started introducing me to her arty friends, and without exception, they all looked down their noses at me. Then I realised that for months I'd been the one to initiate contact, only to be sneered at by them all. So I left it to her. She never rang me and I never saw her again. I grieved, I really did.

At the heyday of our friendship she told me the snail story. When she was small, so small she could only just remember, it was a rainy weekend day, and all the kids were bored and complaining. So after a while their father gave them four buckets of different sizes, the biggest for the eldest and the smallest for the youngest. He then shooed them out into the rainy backyard and told them not to come back in until all the buckets were full of snails right to the top.

That took a long time, and they were drenched and freezing. They brought the buckets of snails back to him, and he led then down the road. They lived close to a really sharp hairpin-bend, and he got them to empty their buckets at the apex of the bend, where traffic from both directions could not see it. There was quite a high pile of snails.

Then he and the kids stood in the pouring rain off the road, and waited for cars to come. Each car would see the pile of snails too late to avoid it, and would hit their brakes and still plough into the pile. After a couple of times, there was snail-slime everywhere, and cars coming round the corner would hit it and slide. He thought that was hilarious.

Judi told me that story round about the time we used to go market-shopping together every weekend, and once she gleefully pounced on a polished boar's skull, complete with tusks. Those things are huge! She was planning on giving it to her father on his birthday as a pointed commentary on his relationship with his children. Instead, oblivious, he took it to work, and put it on his desk, where it made direct eye-contact with his patients during consultations. Imagine! If you were frail and emotionally vulnerable, would you like to be stared down by a huge boar's skull with wicked curled tusks? The man was a sadist.

That was Judi's snail story.

THE PRISON GUARD

The Cape of–no! Jacket of Good Hope was hanging behind the door. The Boots for Kicking You With were outside on the step. Terror Australis was at last home. The only thing she couldn't leave behind was the nickname.

Bare feet on the floor always felt strange. Or, perhaps, not strange so much as vulnerable. But the battlegrounds were well-marked, and they were not inside the home. There was time enough for battle tomorrow.

Right now, it was time for tea. Wet, warm, weak and wonderful, that was tea. Delicate, tender water, delicately and tenderly flavoured, translucent in porcelain. The faces were already beginning to fade away, along with their snarls and profanities.

An empty house always seems colder, in the cool months, than a house which has had life in it during the day, no matter what. Terror took the tea and dropped into her favourite chair, pulling a dirty rug over her lap. There will be time for everything later–now it was time to dream.

She stretched and relaxed. She slumped perfectly still in the recliner, listening to her breathing become shallower and shallower, and with longer intervals between the breaths. She felt the weight of her body and its stillness, then stopped feeling its weight. Where her palms rested on her thighs, the boundaries between hand and leg flickered and became indistinct, as did the boundaries between flesh and furniture. In less than a minute, she was free within her body.

She did a couple of rolls and somersaults inside her body without moving any flesh just for the sheer joy of it, then relaxed again. Inside her flesh-hand, she tightened her inner fist until the knuckles whitened, then spread out her imaginary hand, all without moving her still-limp physical hand. The Three Sisters were already there, and this time it was the one on her left who reached out a hand. She raised her left hand out of her body, held the other's hand, and allowed herself to be pulled out of her body. It was unlike her to be so passive about the process, but it had been a hard day. Each of them kissed her warmly on the lips before leaving: she smelled the spices of one, the baking bread of another and the sheer animal life of the third.

She turned to her own recumbent body for some brief maintenance, and yes, the same issue as yesterday was quite apparent. So she plunged both hands into her abdomen and started pulling out handfuls of bad energy, and throwing it on the floor behind her. It looked and felt like the blackened and crispy twists of dead kelp on the highwater line of a beach long after a storm. It didn't matter how much of it she pulled out, there always seemed to be more. She couldn't see inside her body, but she could feel. She fell into a rhythm: left hand digging in as the right hand was throwing behind, and vice versa. After some time she was no longer able to pull out the deeply satisfying full fists of the stuff, she was getting less and less. Eventually she was running her fingers behind, around and between intestines, uterus, muscle and even bone, with her fingernails scraping and scratching for little remnants to remove.

That would do for today—it would all be back tomorrow, anyway, the problem of working in a toxic environment for money. For now she stretched up and back, exactly as she might have if she had been in her physical body. It was time to go to the Cave, and get started. It was a bit of a climb even without a body, up the irregular slope littered with sand, small loose stones and fallen leaves. The understory was mostly hakea and melaleuca, and as she passed through it, it even whipped her much as it might have if she were in her body, the difference being that it didn't sting or leave scratches.

She would have been panting heavily if she had done the climb physically, but she was silent when she got there. In the entrance of the Cave, as usual, an Aboriginal mother keening over her baby, the mother at once very young and immeasurably ancient, sat cross-legged on the hard earth, weeping. Her red-rimmed eyes looked around her listlessly, barely registering Terror Australis' arrival. Still, it wouldn't be safe to pass her without a gift of some sort. So she placed some fruit and a bowl of the clearest, purest water she could imagine near her. An almost imperceptible nod, and she passed through.

The cave was much as she had left it. The Sydney Sandstone was grey and weathered on the outside, but inside it was young and fresh and yellow.

It looked raw. Carved by tens of millennia of years' worth of winds, and with smaller eddies carving little pockets in its inner walls, the Cave was still far younger than the mother-rock. The world would be a better place if more people thought in Geological Time instead of in Personal Time, Terror Australis mused. Still, that's the inevitable consequence of turning minerals into complex carbon molecules, then into clumps of them that became bigger and bigger organisms, capable of consciousness.

The table was still there, as always. Decades, or hundreds, or thousands, of years ago, a slab of the overhead rock had detached along a weaker mineral fissure, and fallen to the cave floor. It lay there still, with a useable, almost flat surface upwards. Someone had left a daffodil there, lying on the surface, its flower as fresh at the moment it was picked, its plump, green stem still apparently wet from the water of a vase. It was a signature, a signature Terror knew but could not put a name to. She picked it up with gratitude, and left her own customary signature: a tiny silver filigree star. She knew the next out-of-body traveler would find it, and would replace it with their own signature, for her or somebody else to find and replace. It was time to work.

She passed through a fissure into the actual fabric of the rock itself. All around her and through her, the different minerals incorporated in this rock shot their different wavelengths around, announcing themselves. The sensation wasn't really vision or sound—it was more like painless pins-and-needles in multiple flavours. She always enjoyed it, but she wasn't there for fun. Something needed her.

Through the scintillation of different chemical elements, she found it. A lizard-spirit, contorting in agony. She saw the wound, she saw the fibres inside the wound. They were tangled and matted into knots, like long-untended hair. Unlike hair, every fibre was valuable, was alive, could feel pain. Not a one could be broken or lost. And this wasn't one lizard-spirit, or even one lizard species. This was every land-reptile on this baking continent.

Putting her frustration aside, she sat down cross-legged on the sand of the floor of the solid rock, and started untangling. This time she could see what she was doing. She would look for the single end of a whole or broken fibre, then follow it back to where it emerged from the matted tangle. Then she would carefully feed it back into the mat, looking for where it may bulge elsewhere. That found, she would gradually pull it through. Then again. And again, until she had a single fibre free. They needed to run from the head to the tail of the inside of the lizard-spirit, but with the tangle there, there was no room. So she started laying them carefully down in an ordered pile nearby.

After what seemed like hours of work, she had a neat little pile of fibres near her, but the painful tangle seemed no smaller or less complex. She kept working stoically. The lizard-spirit was still, under her ministering fingers. Unconscious? Compliant? Suffering? Tolerant? Lizard-consciousness was different to mammal-consciousness, and she and no way of knowing. What mattered to her was that because it wasn't struggling she could work faster than if she had to restrain it or pacify it.

The work seemed unending, but there came a point where she paused, and stood back to watch, critically. For a moment the lizard shape looked like an Eastern Banded Blue-tongue, writing in agony. It was heaving, trying to regurgitate something. Bloody humans, she suddenly thought. Them, and their fetish for lawns and snail pellets! Don't they know? Yes, the snails are poisoned, but a blue-tongue is not going to say no to free food, and gets poisoned too. And they're not above eating the pellets themselves. Those that don't die after this horrible heaving are probably sterile. And those that are not sterile, have young with incredible defects, who cannot move well enough to feed themselves and escape predators. And if those predators are kookaburras and magpies, the poison just gets passed on into the bird world.

Terror Australis looked at the chain of thoughts. She hadn't been doing the thinking–the lizard-spirit had shown her the thoughts. She tried to shake the sadness out of her enough to continue. And with time, she had more untangled fibres in the pile next to her than tangled ones in her hands. Those that were too irremediably damaged, she put aside elsewhere. The Cave would reabsorb them later, a small, impersonal kindness. The less she left there for resorbtion, the better for everyone and everything.

The beauty of not having a physical body on hand was that you don't ache physically, but you certainly ache, with a down-deep soul-ache. She kept working, until words like "light" and "end" and "tunnel" came to her: at length it seemed possible to imagine that the task would be over. And then, over it was. The last few dozen fibres were really loose and easy to untangle because of the bulk of fibres that had already been removed. The lizard was hollow. Picking up the whole bundle of fibres with both hands, she replaced it in the body-cavity of the lizard. She closed the flesh either side of the wound, pinching it to seal, as a cook might with dough. She righted the lizard onto the ground.

It was still for a moment, then lifted its head slightly and tasted the air. Then it turned its head and looked right inside her. Into her flesh, her bones, her DNA. Right through her DNA, from its pre-mammalian consciousness to her pre-mammalian ancestry. She was seen, properly seen.

And then it was time to go. Out of the rock itself, Terror looked at the cave. There didn't seem to be any housekeeping to do. She glanced at the slab. Her star was still gleaming there, tiny and inconspicuous except to those of her own kind. Home now.

At the cave entry, the grieving Aboriginal mother had eaten some of the fruit and drunk nearly all of the water. The glass bowl had turned into bark, and was full of a wet, grey clay. She said a few words in a forgotten language, but her meaning was clear—Terror respectfully drew near and lowered her head. The woman dipped her fingers in the clay and marked Terror on the forehead, the cheeks, the neck, the shoulders.

Terror Australis lay in her reclining chair for a long time after re-entering her body. Then she went to the deep-freeze and threw a container of leftovers in the microwave, and went and had a long shower, as hot as she could stand. When she emerged she was pink and radiating. The food was defrosted, so she gave it two minutes and ate it straight out of the container with a fork, threw them both in the sink, and went to bed. She needed her sleep. Every prison guard does.

INTERVIEW WITH THE ENBALMER

Interviewer: What is your name?

Embalmer: Eagle-Shepherd'sCrook-Box-Fish.

Interviewer: What do you do for a living?

Embalmer: I take dead bodies, and I make them nice and hard and dry for posterity.

Interviewer: And what do you do for fun?

Embalmer: Not a lot. Who wants to have fun with someone who spends time with dead bodies?

Interviewer: Have you ever worked on someone famous?

Embalmer: When I was a lad I helped my dad with the last pharaoh. I'm already talking to the present incumbent about mummifying him.

Interviewer: That's not many customers. How do you keep in practice?

Embalmer: Well, I don't just do pharaohs, I also do priests and rich entrepreneurs as well. Some of them have some amazing requests! There was one who wanted all his teeth knocked out and replaced with lapis lazuli. I told him I'm an embalmer, not a dentist. But I've got to admit customers other than pharaohs are often thin on the ground.

Interviewer: So how do you maintain your skills?

Embalmer: Well my neighbour, Hyaena-Ibis-Bowl, hates cats. At night he hunts them, and brings them to me to practice on. I get a lot of practice. Let this be a lesson to you: if you love your cat, keep them indoors after dark. Who knows, that might still be sensible advice in four thousand years' time. I've got a bit of a stockpile of cats now. I think I'll start slipping them into customers' burial chambers. Who knows, folks in the future might think that they were loved family pets! I'd have the last laugh, even if deep in posterity.

Interviewer: Fair enough. Have you ever practised on anything else?

Embalmer: Well I was going to do a duck once, but why make a duck dry and hard, when you can throw it on a fire and make it juicy and melt-in-the-mouth soft? So nothing came of that idea.

Interviewer: Getting back to pharaohs, what do you think are important personal qualities in a monarch?

Embalmer: Nice big sinuses and loose brains, mostly, I'm not much interested in politics. I'm also fond of pharaohs who fast a bit before death.

Interviewer: So they are lighter to pick up?

Embalmer: No, I have slaves for the heavy lifting. No, if a pharaoh fasts for a while before they die, that's less of their shit I have to deal with. In a literal sense, you understand.

Interviewer: Okay … What kind of tools do you use?

Embalmer: Different sized knives for opening up different bits of them, a saw for the ribs, pliers for pulling stuff out of the corners, a hoist with pulleys to pick them up and float them in the salt-bath … I have a whole room of different tools, but I never seem to be able to lay my hands on the right one when I need it without a search.

Interviewer: It's a pity they haven't invented multitools yet, isn't it.

Embalmer: Multitools?

Interviewer: You know, a fold-up pair of pliers that fits in your pocket, with all kinds of blades and files and Phillips head screwdrivers and things embedded in the handles.

Embalmer: (bewildered): Phillips … head … screw … thing?

Interviewer: Oh, you know, it's a screwdriver with a tip that fits into those crisscross screws.

Embalmer: …?…

Interviewer: You don't know screws? What do you join bits of wood with?

Embalmer: We usually drill holes in them and use a bloody great mallet to ram a smaller piece of wood in them. <pause> Yeah, just like sex. There's a guy who sells illustrated papyri …

Interviewer: Can we get back to your trade?

Embalmer: Yeah. Do you think they could make one of those multitool thingies with the sizes I'd need my tools to be?

Interviewer: Don't see why not.

Embalmer: But it would need to have a bloody great mallet on it, too, for odd jobs around the home. I don't know if I'd ever use that Phillip thing, though. Never was one for the gay-boys.

Interviewer: Perhaps if you did use a Phillips head screwdriver, you'd end up as a renowned inventor. It might make carpentry easier. Mr Eagle-Shepherd'sCrook-Box-Fish, thank you for your time.

Embalmer: It's a pleasure. And if you ever die, I'll be more than happy to do you.

PESTERING THE WITCH

We all had always known that she was a madwoman. "Madwoman!" we used to chant (from a safe distance) whenever she walked down the road. "Witch! Witchbitch! Miss Johnson is Crazy!" Her long skirt would swing from her wobbly hips as we yelled at her, but she never looked around.

Anthony thought he had seen her naked in her backyard. "Yeah, sure, Anth," we all hooted when he told us, but we listened carefully just the same.

"No kidding," he told us. "I was up in the treehouse mindin' me own business when I seen her. Just strolled out into the yard like she was dressed or something, and watered them strange plants of hers. And she never wears underpants, neither. No kidding."

She had a special bed of plants in her garden to which she paid more attention than the rest, and we were all sure they were witch's herbs—poisons and the like.

Everyone laughed at Anthony and called him a liar. Yvonne eventually decided the matter. "One of us must check," she said. "Anth's not allowed. Someone will have to climb into her garden through the hedge and look at the clothes on her line to see if there are panties. Who wants to do it?"

No one did. We may have joked about her to each other, and shouted taunts to her (from a safe distance from which, I at least hoped, she could not see who was shouting what) but we were all more than a little scared of her. She was the only lady we knew who had grey hair and wasn't even married, let alone a mother or grandmother. She therefore had to be dangerous.

We all shifted in an uneasy silence as Yvonne waited impatiently. Somehow, because she proposed the scheme, no one for a moment imagined that she wasn't going to do it. She looked around us impatiently, for longer than was necessary to ascertain that none of us were going to volunteer. Then she drew a heavy sigh, meant to express exasperation.

"Well, I guess that means we'll have to draw straws for it," she told us importantly. I rejoiced inwardly. Admittedly we usually used this method for the distribution of something good, but even so I had absolutely never drawn the short straw.

As a group we descended on Anthony and Liz's Mum, begging for her famous home-made milkshakes. Within minutes the world's best Mum had the blender whizzing and was putting out paper cups and straws. "Let's take them into the treehouse," Anthony suggested. "We can watch the old bat's backyard from there, and see if she is going to come out naked today." So the six of us crowded up onto the tiny platform, taking turns to hold each other's drinks as we climbed.

As we drank there was no sign that she intended coming out, but we got to see that her washing line was full of clothes. This was a good start, even though it was too far away to say for certain that she had no underwear there.

Then we had six empty paper cups and six straws. It was time. Yvonne collected them with a very grown-up air, and put out a hand to Danny. Silently he handed over his pocket knife. Ceremoniously she hacked off a small part of one straw, dropping the other part to the platform. The tension was rising as we watched in a silence so deep that we could all hear our hearts beating in our ears.

Yvonne carefully wrapped her hands around the lower parts of the straws, fanned them out and held them out to each of us so that we could make a selection. First Dan took a straw. It was uncut. I hung back, knowing that the shortened straw absolutely never came out last. Then Tom took a straw, carefully hiding it from us. "It's against the rules to show until everyone has drawn," he said diffidently. He probably had it. Then Liz, also hiding it. Then Anthony, and me. Everyone but Danny had hidden their straw.

Cut straws absolutely never came out last. I knew I was all right.

"One, two, three, go," said Yvonne, and we all showed our straws. I had it. I had to go.

I could feel the silent sighs of relief around me. I felt teary. "But I'm a girl," I heard myself protesting.

"Why does that matter?"

"Because if I can't get through the hedge, and because if I get caught."

"But she's a lady, and only a girl should look at her underwear."

I had to admit Yvonne had me there. I wouldn't like a boy looking at my underclothes on the line. I thought of something else. "Supposing she hears me?" I asked. "Supposing she comes out in the backyard while I'm there?" I didn't have to say anything about her coming out undressed. I knew they were all thinking it.

"We can keep her busy," piped up Lizzie. Good old Lizzie. So it was decided. I would go around to the hole in the hedge in the Smiths' backyard. They would knock on her front door and keep her talking until I had time enough to go through the hedge, look at the line, and come back out.

Halfway through the gap in the honeysuckle I stuck my head out to make sure she was not around and darted out. There were sheets, towels and clothes on the line, but no trace of either panties or bras. I felt panicky. I suddenly didn't want to tell them that–I felt protective of her for some reason. What could I do?

They would be tittering in the gutter in front of her front window, arguing about who would be the one to knock, when all of them would be standing at the door and it didn't matter. I had time, and home wasn't far away.

I flung myself into the house and tore past my astonished mother into my younger sister's room. I opened her dresser, grabbed the first pair of panties I found and stuffed them into my overalls pocket. I raced out again, pretending not to hear the questions my bewildered mother asked. I didn't have much time. I could only hope she hadn't seen me take the panties.

I raced back breathlessly, scratching myself as I went through the hedge. I could hear the muffled sounds of violent argument from the front of the house, and I knew they would be back soon. Then the house went silent and a moment later I could hear their footsteps approaching along the Smiths' pavement. I could hear the quiet discussion.

When I knew they would be able to see me I came out from my perch in the hedge, twigs and blossoms in my hair, trying to look nonchalant. "Here," I said casually. "I took a souvenir just to prove it." From the depths of my pocket I produced a skinny-arsed little pair of children's red-and-white candy-striped underpants.

SNAIL THE DOG

Hi. My name's Snail, and I'm a dog.

Yeah, I know. I don't look much like a dog. But appearances can be deceiving. I'm in deep cover. This may look like a human body, but let me assure you, it's just my disguise. Deep under all this human-seeming flesh and bones, beats a heart of a dog. Well, not a dog, exactly–it wouldn't be able to cope with human blood and a human body. But behind that human-seeming heart, I'm a dog, I swear I am.

Being a dog comes with a lot of advantages. Humans live in a world of sight and sound. I live in a world of sight and sound, and as much as this inferior nose will let me, smell. Your perfumes, deodorants and aftershaves are painful to me. Your organic smells are more interesting. I can tell with my eyes closed if you are male or female, if you have had sex recently or not, and if you are a female of breeding age, whether you are menstruating or not.

I approve of human hygiene, but even right after a shower, perfectly clean, all humans have an original organic smell, and it always smells better than the chemicals they spray on themselves! And the smells of family members are always similar. Given my human-style education, I've been wondering if dogs with proper dog-noses can smell differences and similarities in DNA.

In my disguise as a human I have to get quite close to you to pick it up, because of the nose I have. To me, the human sense of smell is like a disability, it removes a lot of awareness of the world. But it still works a bit. If I can come close, I can smell if you are sick or well, especially if I am familiar with your base identifying smell. I can smell depression, but not so much happiness. I can smell the passage of time, and get hints of what foods you consistently eat: cheese leaves a pleasant, slightly sour smell on your skin, and seafood leaves an organic, ocean-like smell on your breath. People who drink wine or beer daily, even if they never drink much, always have an acrid smell to them, and I dislike the smell, so for that reason only, out of courtesy to any dogs I might pass, I never drink at all.

Because I'm in a human body, I've been socialized since my earliest memories to behave in at least vaguely human ways. As a toddler, for instance, I discovered quickly that sniffing at the bases of treetrunks or fenceposts was frowned upon, so I no longer do that. Barking, too. But I'm mischievous, and I can't help including barking in my conversation. I might praise the look of a tree's bark, for instance, or mention Bach's Toccata and Fugue in D minor. The word "bark" is ever on my lips.

I long for a proper doggy nose. I had a pet dog once, a mutt called Phlopp. Phlopp used to look at me all the time, puzzled as well as loving. I'm sure he could sense my inner dog, and wondered why it was in a human body. When we walked, I'd let him stop and sniff as often as he wanted. I watch other dog-walkers, and I know that is incredibly rare, but I tell you, a dog needs to stop and sniff! Every time he asked me to slow down and I did, he'd take a long, careful smell.

He could tell what dogs had been near that waystation, how long they stayed, whether they were well or sick, friendly or hostile. He could tell how long it had been since each individual had been there. And only when he had the complete history for that news bulletin resting post since the last rain, would he lay his own storytelling scent onto it as well, to add to its richness for the next dog.

Every so often I wish I were a wolf in human clothing, rather than a dog. When I'm in business meetings and I want to tear out the throat of an idiot, for example. When the moon is bright and I can smell the fog, I just want to run through the trees as fast as my four legs can carry me. When small creatures scurry by me I feel an urge to run them down, while knowing that in this body I can never catch them.

But no, I am a dog, not a wolf. I lie in front of the heater on a reclining chair in winter. I want food on a regular basis, with little or no effort. I scratch—when nobody is looking. I have a horror of fleas. See? Obviously a dog. Could it be any clearer?

I knew I was not human from an early age, possibly from birth. I must have been puzzled that I was in a litter of only one, but I had become used to this by the time I was laying down long-term memories. Being in deep disguise, so deep that even my whole body was that of the disguise, conferred advantages to me. I was always thrilled that nobody around me—except, perhaps, the occasional perplexed dog—knew who I really was. Whatever human-stuff I did, however humanly I behaved, I kept my inner self to myself, and remained undetected.

I did the human-family-stuff, once, long ago. When the pregnancy was confirmed, I told my doctor that my wife was probably carrying twins, simply because it was inconceivable to me that I might have fathered a litter of only one. Nevertheless, it was only one. Throughout his childhood, I kept a careful eye on him, watching for signs of an inner dog. Sniffing, scratching, showing an interest in people's nether regions and an obsession with his own.

Nothing. Nada. The horrible truth dawned on me gradually. I was a dog inside a human body, and I had mated with a human. In my son, there was no dog left. He was entirely, completely human. I had failed him even before he was born. I had given life to a human.

He liked dogs, I made sure of that. There were always devoted hounds around, wanting to be patted, scratched, walked and fed. He was happy to do some of the walking and feeding, less happy to pick up the dog-eggs that successive dogs left lying around in the yard. But was he one of them? Nope.

I was hopelessly devoted to my son. DNA saw to that, chaining me to him by the heart, making me have an interest in everything about him, making me want to smooth his path through life. I did all the things that conventional human parents do. But I really missed lying on a floor with multiple puppies—or even just one puppy—crawling all over me, biting them when it got annoying. It was never to happen.

And the older he got, the more human he was. By contrast, the older I got, the less human I was. By the time he was a teen, I was hanging out for him to grow a brain, grow an income and move out of home, so that I could live a more natural and more doglike life. I hung on by the fingernails for years, waiting for it to happen.

And one day it did. He packed his bags, filled a car and left. I was finally free to live my own best life! Having spent a lifetime conditioned by humans and the human world to behave in humanlike ways, it took me a while. I started ignoring the morning alarm. I showered and dressed when I damn well pleased, instead of to some human timetable. I lounged, half-asleep, in my recliner for hours and hours in the evening. I ate at increasingly irregular times, triggered not by the awareness of mealtimes, but by suddenly remembering there was food in the kitchen. I snuffed at the aroma of my own slept-in bedclothes in the morning.

But, dammit, the body stayed human-like. And there were bills to pay (not very important) and food to buy (hugely important), so I still had to keep making money.

Outside of doing the necessary human-things, I allowed my inner dog out more and more often. If I were restless at midnight for example, I'd get up, dress enough not to attract unwanted human attention, and prowl on foot around the local area. I'd stop and look at random things. I'd breathe deeply and very slowly, so that airborne chemicals—the basis of smell—would have more chance to be detected by my flawed human nose. And I would never, never howl.

But barking was something I occasionally did to great effect. As I child I practiced barking with a human mouth, and I became quite good at it, if I was doing a small-yappy-dog bark. I never mastered a big-relaxed-mutt bark, my vocal equipment was all wrong. Once when I was alone in the house and I could hear someone trying to open one of the windows, I barked enthusiastically, and they swore and left.

Another time, after the divorce my son and I were on a driving holiday, and one morning we went for a walk around a small country town, a charming place. As we approached a house with a pretty cottage garden behind a fence, a small yappy thing, a Maltese terrier, came out and barked at us through the fence. In response, I growled back, and let out a little warning-yip, then a flurry of barking even better than his. The dog shut up and backed off, terrified and confused. On our way back, approaching the same house, the same dog came out to bark at us. Instead of barking back, I spoke to him in Human, saying "Yeah, yeah, you've already done all that." To my son's astonishment, the dog shut up and backed right down.

Ironically, although I can only do a little-dog-bark, I'm great at a large-wolf-howl. Sadly, I don't live in a country with a population of wild wolves for me to seek out and freak out with my howling. Perhaps I should try it in dingo territory. Howling terrifies humans, though, so as I said before I try to keep it to a minimum.

Dingos are interesting dogs. Phlopp had some dingo in him. The only place you could see it was in his mouth: dingos and part-dingos have normal jaws, but small mouth-openings, so their lips don't open as far back against their jaws as you think they should. If you don't believe me, really pay attention next time. He, however, was all lapdog, just content to be warm and fed and loved.

His flatulence was something to be believed. Every human I knew including my child thought it was foul, and superficially, so did I. But I enjoyed sniffing it up because it was so interesting. I could smell the differences between him on canned food, and dry food, and home-made dog food. Not better or worse smells, and not very different smells, but interesting variants. And that's one of the crucial dog-abilities: detecting interesting variants on standard smells.

Just yesterday I was walking along the road smelling the sunlight and feeling it on my back, and a friend driving by offered me a lift. I got in and immediately regretted it. The car had the acrid smell of panic. As we drove along, I asked what was wrong. Nothing, I was told. And she herself smelled peaceful. But there was a distinct smell of panic in the car.

Casually, I asked about her teenagers. Mitchell had a driving lesson that went wrong last night, she told me. She was trying to get him to get up his night hours and his rainfall hours, and last night fitted the bill. A traffic light turned orange, and he was close. She told him to accelerate through it, because they were too close to it and the road was wet and slippery.

The only problem with that, was the person waiting in the side street wasn't looking at the road or their own traffic lights, but was looking at the glare of Mitchell's traffic light so they could get the jump. And they did. As soon as Mitchell's light turned orange they shot out into the intersection. She didn't have time to give instruction, he didn't have time to listen and obey. Faced with headlights bearing down on him and nowhere to go, he jumped the car up onto the curb.

He stopped the car in a panic, and saw a woman on the pavement, screaming. He was convinced he'd run over her child. He himself was screaming and weeping, and it took forever to calm him down, make sure the woman was all right and establish she didn't have a child who had gone under their wheels, and get the car off the curb back into the road.

He refused to drive home, and hours afterwards, he was sitting in front of the TV, shaking.

So it was his panic I smelled, in my friend's car the next day.

When I was between cars I used buses a lot, which I hated because they were horrible, having spent all their time being full of horrible people who left their chemical traces behind them. There were two bus companies servicing the area I lived in, and the buses of both companies were air conditioned, and both companies put air freshener in their air conditioning.

One of the companies, their air conditioning smelled like the chemicals you'd expect, but the other smelled like sweetened sewage. I used to sit there, knowing in my head it wasn't, but with my nose telling me something different. I used to take long, slow breaths, trying to identify why an artificial fragrance would be so close to sewage. After a few months of riding on their buses I think I worked it out. I believe the blend of fragrances they used worked out at exactly the same pH as raw sewage, and that I was smelling the pH.

I'm quite used to smelling sex on people even when they've showered carefully afterwards, and it's a slightly different smell on each person, or each couple. One day at university I was sitting next to a fellow student who always had an active sex-life, and his smell was different. Because he smelled like sex but different, I asked if he's broken up with his girlfriend. No, he said. Later, he was telling me all about his drunken night out. He told me all the details—except that he had actually had sex with the woman he was flirting with. In that ignorant human way, he fancied that I couldn't tell!

Having an inner dog is almost as good as having hidden cameras, in that sense. But I'm always hampered by the fact that I do all my smelling through a human nose. Everything I can smell you can, too, because the hardware is no different. It's just that my inner dog is used to regarding smell as the most important sense, whilst humans regard it as the least important sense, so you're culturally set up to disregard small differences in aroma.

Imagine a life where I had a proper nose, one that works the way I've always suspected my nose should work. I could have had all sorts of different careers. I could have been Police Officer Snail, poking around a crime scene, identifying the direction an offender left in, sensing their

DNA in the air faintly, and more strongly around wherever they fled to, or identifying by smell alone just how much over the limit a drunk-driver was, or exactly what narcotics someone had taken.

Or I could have been an exceptional diagnostician in a hospital, Dr Snail, known to be eccentric but brilliant, sniffing out different bacterial or viral infections, knowing what organ was overworking or underworking by smell, sensing the faint, musty odour of tumours. Or a great psychologist, smelling the emotions that my patients are covering up, and forcing them to confront what they most want to deny, and to begin dealing with it.

But no. I don't have a dog-style nose, because I am in one of these dreadful human-style bodies. Instead, the canine soul in this body can sense that an upright stance and a flat sense of smell is just wrong, without being able to do anything about it. Because of this, I used to see myself as disabled, disadvantaged.

Now, I'm starting to feel differently. It's really just a matter of perspective. Lately, I am choosing to see myself as being in the most perfect of disguises. As being in deep cover. I am a dog-agent, a dog-spy, roaming around as freely in the human world as if I were one of them. And none of the humans realise I'm not!

This gives me a heady sense of freedom, an intoxicating sense of triumph, because I am undetected and know that I will never be detected. After all, most disguises can be stripped off after a while, but my disguise is deeply layered into me, it is the very flesh of my body, so nobody will ever be able to see through it. No human, anyway. Any dog worth his salt can smell right through the disguise.

So I will continue roaming around in the human-world: a dog in disguise, a dog-agent, a dog-spy. I will sniff out everything my defective human nose can. I will store up memories of the smells of people, places, events. And when it is time for me to go to the great kennel in the sky, I will take all that olfactory data back to base with me.

THE WEDDING

At last it's happened. It's too late, now, to back out. After all the mistakes, all the judgements, this is where I end up, slowly pacing up an aisle in a strange place dedicated to gods I do not believe in. Fitting, somehow: I am marrying a man I cannot love in a place sacred to gods I cannot accept.

The dress is too tight, too horrible, too heavy, a travesty in satin and lace designed to make old women go "aaah" and to look bizarre and dated in photo albums. I'm in matching white satin slippers which make my feet sweat, and I slide around in them insecurely, uncertain whether I will fall over my own sweat. The music is horrible: Mendelssohn played badly on a shockingly out of tune instrument by someone who hates the music and plays by rote.

I take a step.

I am trapped. The press of people around me is designed to prevent my getting away. On either side of me, the people sitting in the pews have risen and are all looking at me with their teeth pulled back in grimaces designed to look like fond smiles but actually looking like instinctual animal threats. Their flesh is too close, and prevents me swerving and running away. Their gazing eyes are recorders of evidence for my conviction later.

How do I get away?

In case I spin around and leave the way I came, a press of my very best friends are following me, playing traitor, officiating at the death of my life, forcing me to marry because everyone expects it of me. They too wear satin, in their case a deep, shimmering blue, but they are not sweating and tears are not leaking from the corners of their eyes and making dark rivulets forced down and sideways into the sweaty hair.

I take another step.

I am carrying a bouquet of jasmine. It twists in my sweaty hands. I hate jasmine. It stops me breathing. "Nonsense! Jasmine will look good with the gown," I am told by my forceful European mother who is always more perfect than I am. So I am carrying jasmine. It coats my tongue, clots in my windpipe, makes my stomach churn and my lungs shrink painfully.

Even as a free young thing I hated jasmine in Chinese tea: when a plump and lovely curly-haired Eurasian seduced me (shocking me completely at how I responded), the tea we had been drinking for hours and hours was oolong, unflavoured with this detestable bloom. I want to drop the bouquet, trample it, horrify everyone. I want to see it mashed into the flagstones. I want to know that all jasmine is extinct throughout the known world.

If I do anything to the jasmine, my mother will kill me, quite literally. She has hidden weapons. She always has hidden weapons. She is sitting right there, watching me, watching every move, making sure I don't do the wrong thing. If I break script, I give myself five hours, maximum, before she has me locked up in either a police cell or a psychiatric ward.

But if I do anything to the jasmine, the rising wave of perfume from the crushed petals will suffocate me, and I will die in the miserable horror of this smell before she has a chance to do anything to me.

I take another step.

I have time to spare. I need to know in my last moments why I am here, why I am doing this insane thing. I think it's because two years ago two fat men in motorcycle boots, blue jeans, white helmets, black leather jackets and almost identical beards walked into my living room to visit my flatmate. I think it was because one of them came back another time to visit me, and was both tender and funny. I think it was because I felt ugly. I think it was because a girlfriend of mine had told me he was in line for a directorship of a large international business and that while he was already prosperous, he would be totally loaded some day.

Did I really think marrying him for his money would make me happy, when I have steadfastly disallowed him to pay my bills or buy expensive presents out of pride and appearances? Did I really think marrying him for his love of me would make me happy when I didn't love him back but only had a shaky resolve to selflessly make him happy? Did I really need yet another comedian in my immediate family? What on earth was I thinking?

And why, Gods, why in summer? I know I get sweat-abrasions between my thighs in summer. I know I smell in summer no matter what chemicals I coat myself with. I know my fingers and feet puff up in summer. Well then. Perhaps if one has to do something incredibly stupid, summer is a good season to do it in.

I take another step.

Perhaps I am only here to spite his mother, who said he'd never amount to anything and would never be able to hold onto a good woman. (*Am* I a good woman, who tells lies with every look, touch and word?) Perhaps I am here to make her happy in her declining years. Perhaps I am here because his brother beats his children, and the family owes the world a few happy kids.

I move my head to the other side, but only by a few centimetres as my neck is frozen. Out of the corner of my eye, I can see the ridiculous netted hat his mother has bought to match the bridesmaids.' She has spent a huge amount on clothes she will never wear again.

I spent thousands on a dress that I'll never wear again, too, and shouldn't be wearing now. If I really had to get married, I should have been wearing a scarlet mini-skirt trimmed with black lace. I should have hung around just long enough for the photographs, then said "no" at the altar. Really, really loudly. I should have asked the Best Man to get him drunk and put him on a flight to Greenland with no cash, cards or return ticket. What does Greenland do with illegal immigrants—imprison them for years on end as we do? Perhaps he would live in an igloo for seventy years and eat raw sealmeat.

I wish I could live in an igloo for seventy years and eat raw sealmeat. It sounds like a bargain to me.

I feel an illogical well of longing rise up in me. The plump and lovely Eurasian girl with the curly black hair that felt so good in my fingers is on the other side of the continent now, following her yuppie dream of promotion, pay and package deals. How could I begrudge her that? How could I ask her to stay? And she never asked me to give away my career path and fringe benefits to follow her. I would probably have refused, anyway.

We kissed chastely, hugged, and laughed a lot at the airport departure lounge, every smile cutting my heart to shreds. When she finally went through the gates, she did so without a backward look, and the tears flooded down my face. I went to the bar, grabbed a double brandy, dropped some uncounted notes somewhere, and gulped it down as I made my way to the observation deck. Was that plane taxiing out, her plane? I watched it anyway in the cold winter air, howling my eyes out like a three-year-old in a tantrum.

I don't know why I am thinking about all this now. Perhaps a plane has just flown over this consecrated place, violated by my unbelieving presence. She would never be trapped, not the way I am. She knew who she was and what she wanted. By contrast, I never dared to reach out and take anything, not even her—she had to reach out and take me. And now she is far away, and the only person willing to reach out and take me is an overweight bikie in an uncomfortable tuxedo, looking back at me and smiling anxiously, trying to make an eye-contact that I am desperately avoiding.

One last step. There is no room around me, no room to move. I cannot go anywhere. I stop walking. The music stops. The bridesmaids, those traitor friends, fan themselves out on one side of me—and suddenly there is space behind me.

And before I know what is happening, I whirl around in my slippery slip-on slippers and run, run inside my stained and constricting satin, flinging the hated jasmine away from me as far as I can in the direction of my mother. One of my slippers falls off and I hear a howl a lot like my own voice as I recover from slamming against the door-jamb.

Stumbling out, I keep running, running over the penetrating gravel that I no longer care will cut my feet up, running deeper and deeper into the comforting sunlight of insanity.

THE PAGAN SPEAKS

I'm not really going to tell you a story, I'm going to tell you about a few meditations I did. There's the one where I met the Ferryman, the one where I met the Green Man, and the one where the Grey Lady took me to the centre of the galaxy and taught me science. I might or might not talk about the failed lesson, too, the one I didn't get.

The word Witch gets traded around a lot, especially in my generation. I'm twenty-six and, certainly on the net, the young self-proclaimed witches you tend to see, are clueless and haven't the first idea. So I call myself a Pagan, as the older generation mostly do. I've spent a lot of time working on myself with meditation and ritual, and forming Otherworldly contacts.

I have a teaching figure that comes to me in meditation and teaches me stuff. I call her the Grey Lady or the Grey One. it seems more respectful than asking for a personal name. She's one of my regulars. She's taught me how to go out of body, how to lucid dream, how to build non-physical temple-space, all sorts of things. She's a solid contact.

One night when my boyfriend was asleep next to me and I was just meditating a bit before I was planning on going to sleep, she came to me. She took me by the left hand, and gently tugged me out of my body. We walked up through the ceiling, out into the night sky above my and my neighbours' places, and climbed higher and higher, while feeling as if we were just walking on a flat surface.

Soon the ground was a long way away, and we were walking on a soft, thin layer of cirrus cloud, its upper surface shining in the starlight. We went past the moon, out of the solar system. It's not as if we were moving huge distances, it was as if we are moving at a comfortable rate, but getting bigger and bigger so that each step was taking us further.

We walked a long way, through a lot of space. At one point we stopped, and the Grey One put a neutron star in one of my hands, and a brown dwarf in the other, so that I could really feel the difference in weight, texture, heat and structure. Then she took them out of my hands, and put them both where they belonged. Funny thing was, although I had a sense of the high temperatures I didn't get burnt, and although I could feel the immense gravitational forces, I didn't get crushed.

We walked further and further towards the centre of the galaxy, the Grey One occasionally pointing out landmarks as we went. I had the feeling that was so that I could find my own way home. We've all seen pictures of spiral galaxies, and are told our Milky Way galaxy looks like that, with like a big ball of stars in the centre and two spinning curved arms radiating out and around it. Well, when you actually get up there, it looks entirely different. It's more like a ball of stars in the middle and a flat disc around it, kind of like a vinyl LP with a ping pong ball in the centre. And a huge, pale, blown-up loop of far distant stars around that, like a ring around Saturn at an odd angle.

And as you get closer and closer, the disc isn't a disc, it's incredibly wide, with many stars stacked on top of each other and huge spaces between them. So more like a gigantic cylinder. We had been walking through this all the time. As we got closer, the ball of stars in the middle spread out, so it really was dark, with lots of space between the stars. But that space was hot and, I dunno, bent or warped somehow. Just really strange.

It took us a long time to get right in there, and when we were, the space we were occupying felt small and cramped and really twisted. The Grey One waved her hand in a complicated gesture, and cleared a little patch of normal space for us. She indicated that I was to sit down, and I suddenly found a little chair and desk, the kind kids in primary school have. I sat down. There was a massive green chalkboard in front of me. The Grey One picked up a piece of chalk and started talking.

She said: "The universe is like a doughnut," and she drew a massive circle on the chalk board, probably two metres across. And she drew it with one quick movement. We all know circles drawn like that are not circular, they're oval, and their ends don't meet up. But even though she drew it so casually, it was perfect. A scientist could have measured it, and it would have been perfect.

Then she said: "And God is the hole in the centre of the doughnut." She drew a smaller circle inside it, again quickly, and again, perfectly. And suddenly the whole diagram looked very doughnutty. I could almost feel the heat of it, and smell the cinnamon.

She went on to explain to me: "A doughnut without a hole is just an unpleasant, heavy, deep-fried cake. But with a hole, it suddenly becomes magical. Less soggy, less sodden in oil, less heavy, and much, much more tempting. In the same way, the universe of the scientists, the universe without God, can function perfectly well without God. And God, like the hole in the doughnut, is nothing. But put God into the universe, and like the doughnut, the universe is suddenly shiny, attractive, interesting and meaningful. God is, in fact, the hole in the doughnut, the doughnut that is this universe."

Such a simple idea, but it blew my mind at the time. I sat there a few minutes, digesting the new idea, chewing it over. Richard Dawkins is right - the universe needs no god. But like a fried cake that is given a hole, a universe with a god is a much nicer place to live. She didn't say that out loud and nor did I, but that's where my thoughts took me.

And when I got there, she said "Class dismissed." I stood up and left the little bit of cleared space, into the wild, tangled space in the centre of the galaxy. Then, remembering all the landmarks, I slowly picked my way home. When I got close, Earth looked like a pretty opal lying on a piece of black velvet, not quite round, with blue, green and brown fire, with tiny diamonds studded along the coastlines, with beautiful white cottonwool swirling over it. It didn't take long to find Australia, then my town, my roof and my body. Then I went into a deep sleep until morning.

The story about the Ferryman also happened during that relationship, and even in the very same bedroom. I was lying on the bed meditating, and Corey was at the desk, typing away at his screenplay. I wasn't planning to go anywhere special, but I found myself in a silver landscape. Silver ground, a silver river near me, a silver sky overhead, and dark rounded hills on the other side of the river. They looked to be covered in scrub. It was beautiful and otherworldly.

I was walking among dark mangrove trees growing out of this silver swamp at the edge of the river. I saw a dark jetty. I walked out onto the jetty. I could feel every one of the irregular boards, every one of the heads of the rusty rivets that held it together, even a splinter or two. It felt really tangible under my feet. Two or three metres before the end of the jetty, I stopped and waited.

A few minutes later, to my right, so, what? Probably the north-east? A little black dot appeared on the river at a great distance, and got nearer. It resolved into a, well not a barge, more a flat-bottomed and square-bowed dinghy, barges are larger, aren't they? This was only a little bigger than a regular dinghy. On the back a man in a long cloak with a hood was standing, poling it forwards towards me with a long, black pole.

He stopped at the end of the jetty, the barge perfectly aligned with it. He looked at me, I looked at him, at his empty hood. I knew who he was. I also had absolutely no emotions—no fear whatsoever. Then he held out one hand. It was an invitation. If I were to take his hand, he would help me onto the barge, then pole us across to the dark hills. I would never come back. I would at last know exactly what lies after death, something I am really curious about. I mean - I know what I believe - but to KNOW!

And—here's then compellingly tempting bit—I would get to die with absolutely no illness or pain! I immediately knew that if I took his hand, my death would be instant and pain-free, and on autopsy they wouldn't be able to work out what happened. That was the deal. But if I refused, I might live a much longer life, but I would certainly have a more painful death. That was also the deal.

And all the time, Corey was typing, I could hear him. The offer to leave was very tempting indeed—I needed him to call me back to life. I needed him to psychically realise I was in trouble, and reach over and touch me. Or say my name. Or even just stop typing, that would have done it. Just some indication that his psychic abilities, of which he's proud, actually work when I need them the most.

But no. He was no help whatsoever. I had to decide whether to live or die by myself, without help. And I'm here now, so that tells you what I eventually decided. The Ferryman poled his boat back to where he came from without me, and I know I won't see him again until I have no option of refusal.

The Green Man was earlier, before I met my partner. I was living in Darwin at the time, enjoying the Dry Season, but not enjoying the Wet Season at all. I had just had my twenty-first. One night I came home from a friend's place a little drunk, and as I got ready for bed I noticed I was spinning pleasantly. I knew that when I was spinning was a really good point for out of body work, so when I lay down, instead of going to sleep, I allowed myself to be spun out of my body.

I found myself walking down a forest path. It wasn't really Australian bushland, at least, not like any area I've lived in. Tall, straightish trees, European ones - I think I recognised elms and perhaps beeches, but I'm no expert. The understorey was easy to walk through even without paths, it was soil covered by old, rotting fallen leaves from last season, with the odd fern unfurling or a small clump of something grassy with yellow or mauve flowers. It was warm and humid, and the trees had dark green summer leaves, not pale green spring leaves.

I walked and walked. I could hear dried leaves and tiny twigs crackling underfoot, and I could smell the smell of warm, damp soil and compost, with a hint of mushrooms somewhere. The sun fell between the trees onto my back, which was lovely and warm in a really physical way ... but I had no shadow in front of me, so I was obviously successfully out of body.

I probably walked for half an hour, watching the ants on the tree-trunks rushing up and down, and sometimes in a diagonal shaft of light I'd see clans of tiny flying insects doing a social dance that seemed like pure joy. But there were no reptiles or birds, all animal life was small, and exclusively consisted of arthropods.

Up ahead of me was a pool of intense sunlight. As I got closer, I saw it was made by a place where the trees were further apart, and closer still, I realised that this was because two trees had fallen, clearing the way for all that extra sunlight. I walked into that space. It wasn't regular in shape at all - just a wound or a tear in the irregular non-pattern of the forest.

The two fallen trees lay almost parallel to each other. One had a thicker trunk than the other, and was less decomposed. Its base was propped up a bit by its roots, stopping that end of the trunk from touching the ground. At the other end, some of its branches had broken, and that end was lying flat, so the trunk had a slope to it. The other one had fallen more than one season earlier, I think, and had started rotting. It was soft and spongy, lots of different fungi sprouting out of it, and lots of insect-holes in it.

I sat on the newer trunk, my feet on the older, more rotten one. I knew this was no time for impatience. I waited. I smelled all the smells around me. They were all foresty and many of them were smells of decomposition, but good smells of decomposition. I felt the touch of the air on my skin, cooler or warmer in fine strands and by tiny degrees of temperature, flowing over me like water.

The trees as individuals, all knew I was there. The forest as a whole, knew I was there. The more empty my mind was of thoughts, the more still my body was, the more the forest accepted me. After a while it was hard to tell where I ended and the forest began. After a bit more of a while, it was unnecessary to even notice this merging of myself with the forest.

When the process was almost complete and I was only just myself, the Green Man walked towards me. His skin was the colour and texture of cypress bark. His bare forearms and lower legs were thin, slightly twisted branches. His long fingers and toes were twigs, with growth nodes at all the joints. His facial features were made out of a combination of twigs, leaves and growth nodes. His clothes, hair and beard, such that they were, were made of leaves. All kinds of leaves. All different shapes and shades of green.

He sat next to me, his thigh just touching me, and the smell of the forest became stronger. His leg didn't have the warmth of humans, it had the coolness of raw timber. We sat in silence, both of us looking forward. I don't know who moved first, but after a while we had both twisted our bodies so that we were still sitting next to each other, but facing each other. To look at him directly was to drown in amber, nectar, compost and photosynthesis. To be looked at by him was to be known in your entire nakedness by the whole of the planet-wide plant kingdom.

He spoke. His voice was like the rustling of leaves, and like the wind through the hanging needles of she-oaks, and like the creaking of branches in the storm. With one of his cool, wooden hands he picked up one of mine, and his other hand, curled closed, placed something in my palm that felt rounded and smooth. He closed my hand into a fist and kept holding it between both of his.

"Take this in memory of me. Keep this in memory of me."

Then everything faded, me included. I ended up in a deep, dreamless sleep. When I woke up in the morning I wasn't hung over at all, and the sunlight was streaming over my bed from the curtains which I had forgotten to close. The room smelled mostly of sweaty female, but I could still catch hints of a foresty, compost smell.

I opened my eyes. The same hand was still curled in a loose fist. I sat up, remembering, and carefully opened my fingers, expecting to find nothing. What I found was a perfect acorn, one without a blemish. It was a gift from the Green Man, that I took in memory of him and was meant to keep in memory of him. It had crossed dimensions from a mental space into a physical space. It was a sacred gift.

Yes, I know. I was awed.

But time passed. I still knew it was a sacred gift. But I got greedy. My thought-process went like this after a few weeks: if one magical acorn is special, imagine the awesomeness of a whole lot of magical acorns!

I went on the net, and carefully researched how to grow oak trees from acorns: what kind of conditions they like, the best soil composition, what season, how deep to bury them, all that sort of stuff. And I went to a lot of trouble to give that magical acorn just the right growing conditions. I loved it and nurtured it. And nothing happened.

I thought a lot about that acorn, over the years since. In fact, I grieved for it, I cried and everything. It left a hollow inside me that I still can't really fill. I should have known that a magical acorn given to me by a god when I was in a magical space, was not an acorn for growing! Ages after I planted it, I dug into the pot and ended up sifting the soil, looking for the tiniest fragment of decomposed acorn, and didn't find any.

The moment I got greedy and tried to multiply the gift, the Green Man took it back to the Otherworld, and left me with nothing but the knowledge that I betrayed his trust. I've been trying to make it up to him by scattering seed and picking up litter ever since, but it's not enough. And it will never be enough.

And the lesson I didn't get? When I woke up, I tried to draw the scene of that lesson, and emailed the drawing to a friend of mine. She swears it was the Matthews Building, in the University of NSW. Again, in a meditation, I found myself in a lecture hall. Down on the stage was a man with curly brown hair wearing brown cords and a yellow shirt, speaking to a room full of all sorts of people.

I was aware that he was telling us the deepest, most sacred of all the world's spiritual secrets. I had my notepad and was trying to scribble notes— it seemed to be pre-technology, or perhaps mine had failed. As he talked, he casually stuck his hand in his trouser pocket, pulled out a bright orange ping-pong ball, and tossed it with a flick of the fingers, into the audience.

It bounced all over the place, never losing speed, changing direction sharply and erratically. It became a small, orange imp with the zoomies, as well as being still an orange ping-pong ball. The group divided into two: there were those who valued his teachings, who kept their heads down and kept taking notes, and tried to ignore the fuss. And there were the others, who got caught up in the fun, and bounced all over the hall, chasing after the ball, trying to predict its unpredictability, laughing and shouting, and racing after it.

The lecturer kept talking, kept giving out the deep secrets of the universe. I couldn't take part in the fun, because the information was just too important. But I was too easily distracted, and I couldn't keep my head down, either, and keep writing notes. I lost out on the information, and I lost out on the fun.

These are just some of the things that have happened.

A LOVE AFFAIR AND A FLIGHT

This happened in the 1980s, when my mother was young. She decided to go on the trip of a lifetime. She had just completed her first university degree, one with a double in history and archaeology. She always loved old things, which accounts for, well, all of her husbands, really, my Dad and the others after him.

But back then she was single, and flushed with the success of getting a degree. But I'm not sure it really counts, not like my science-meteorology degree, which was hard. During her second and third year she had volunteered to go on digs in South Australia looking at early human remains and the way the first people dealt with burials in that region.

Nowadays they'd have a first nations person or two watching, and they'd rebury the remains with ceremony after they had been studied, but it was a different time back then, and she saw nothing wrong with digging up bits of people, putting them through a laboratory, then storing them in the university or a museum or something. Like I said, a different time.

She showed me photographs of her and her friends in academic weeds, smiling broadly and holding scrolls. She looked young and a bit gormless and really not like the kind of girl you'd date, but she also didn't look like someone who would ultimately end up looking like my mother, either. She looked happy.

After her graduation, one of her tutors got in touch with her, telling her he was going on a dig in Turkey to investigate the remains of some town or other that had been involved in the Persian War or the Punic War or something like that. Anyway, it was a very famous conflict in ancient times, and they thought they found an important site.

Of course, she said yes. She probably didn't even take a breath before answering. She organised a passport and threw herself on her parents' mercy for some spending-money, and made the same plane out with her tutor.

They spent two nights in a hotel, looking at plans and site photographs with the leaders of the dig, who were from all kinds of countries, so the room was full of people who spoke broken English, and a few translators as well. Then they went out to site.

My mother didn't like it very much. They slept in tents on the bare ground, and didn't have any washing facilities or even toilets–needing a toilet meant walking out of the campsite with a hand-shovel and some loo paper, and no chance of any privacy. She loved the actual work, though–painstakingly scratching at the ground, and removing anything at all for cleaning up and examination later. Even though she was young, she ended up very stiff and very sunburnt, because she just kept working through the optional breaks.

Things got a bit better when she fell in love with an English archaeologist. As a senior on the dig, he was one of the few who had a tent to himself and a camp-bed, so at night she used to sneak into his tent for a few hours. Then one day he got a call on the radio, and made an announcement to the whole camp. His wife had just given birth.

He was ecstatic. My mother, who hadn't known he was married and had fantasised about their future life together, was crushed. She cried for two days, then left the dig. She bought a ticket home, rang her parents, and got on a flight.

Her flight out had been taken in a state of anticipation and high excitement, and every moment of it–her first ever flight–had been wonderment. The flight home was miserable. Presenting her ticket and checking in her bags was miserable. Getting checked over at customs was miserable. Finding her cheap seat down the back of the plane was miserable. Belting herself in was miserable. Waiting for what seemed like hours for the plane to taxi away from the terminal was miserable. Then the wait at the end of the strip before the takeoff was miserable.

She managed not to sob, but she couldn't stop her eyes from leaking at the corners. The plane was very full–she felt embarrassed. She kept her head turned slightly, looking out into the back of one of the jet engines mounted on the wing, into its infernal red centre. She wished her body was in there, burnt to a crisp and blown out the back as the finest dust.

A female flight attendant was doing the safety demonstration. She tried to pay attention, but not a word the girl said stuck in her head. After an interminable wait, the engines finally started roaring on a higher, more hysterical note. Slowly, slowly the plane crept forward, then accelerated, thrusting her back into her chair.

She felt the exact moment when the plane's tyres left the ground–the floor of the plane and the seat below her suddenly felt insubstantial. The nose tilted up sharply, the plane screaming as they climbed. It sounded the way she felt, she thought. They must have climbed through a cloud; it looked like fog outside the window, then was gone in an instant. They levelled off, and the seatbelt light went out.

The flight attendants went from row to row, offering magazines and drinks. She said no to magazines, wine and coffee. She accepted a chilled bottle of water, but it turned out to be Evian–undrinkable. She put it aside, still sealed. She sat there, her temple against the inner layer of reinforced glass of the window, staring into the fiery, howling engine. It was the only thing that made any sense right now.

On his way back after finishing his rounds, a male flight attendant paused next to her, bent over, and whispered "He's probably thinking of you, too, love," then straightened up and kept walking. She realised he was being kind, but his kindness did not touch her. She knew "he" was not thinking of her, and hadn't thought of her since the moment he found out about the birth.

Time passed. Her feelings did not. She refused a meal. She refused alcohol. She hadn't drink her mineral water, and was dehydrating, so she asked for fruit juice. They brought her a bottle of some highly sweetened fruit-flavoured confection–she wet her mouth with it.

She knew there would be a stop-off before they got back to Australia. She wasn't interested. She would stay put. She wasn't enthusiastic about roaming airports and buying duty-free. The pilot had made a few announcements during the flight, but she hadn't paid attention. The only things that held her attention were the red-roaring in her heart and in the engine.

A female attendant came up to her. "I know you're travelling alone and you're not feeling good, Miss," she said, "and the pilot and co-pilot were wondering if you'd like to sit in the cockpit, in one of the seats behind them. You'll get to have a much better view of the landing, and you'll get to see what the boys do. It's not often they offer that chance to someone."

Yeah, why not, she thought, it couldn't be any worse, could it? Aloud, she used her manners and thanked the attendant, who led her into the cockpit, introduced her to the crew, and made sure she was securely belted in–apparently all people in cockpits were seatbelted at all times. The pilot and co-pilot glanced over, smiled, then got on with what they were doing.

She was amazed at what a great view the cockpit windows gave. It was pretty-much a god's-eye-view of the world. The pilot and the person on the other end of the radio were talking constantly, in low, calm tones, mostly in a code of numbers and letters. Both the pilot and co-pilot were concentrating hard on the job at hand.

The plane banked sharply, turning in the air. She saw the horizon dip, and saw sea turn to land and turn to sea again. It looked impressive. She watched the sea and the edge of the land rush up towards them as they came in for the landing. It was better than impressive, it was fantastic. Then she could see the control tower at the airport–the person's voice that she could hear was sitting in that tower right now! She was absorbed. She had almost forgotten her own pain.

"Now!" said the pilot, and the co-pilot moved something sharply, she couldn't see what, over his shoulder. The runway rushed up to meet them. There was a bump and another as they hit the tarmac, bounced, and hit again. They seemed, to my Mum, to be still moving really fast. They went right to the end of the runway, then slewed around to the left, then stopped.

The pilot opened his mike. "Ladies and gentlemen, we have made it down onto the ground safely. Please stay in your seatbelts until we flick the light. We will get you to disembark safely as soon as possible."

The cockpit door opened, and she could hear applause and cheering. A flight attendant came to get her. She was confused. "What happened?"

The attendant smiled warmly. "We didn't crash, due to these two skilled gentlemen."

"Crash? Why did you move me here?"

And here comes the punchline. "It wasn't because you were travelling alone, Miss. It was because your seat was right in the emergency exit, and if we needed to deploy the inflatable slide you would have been in the way. We thought it best to get you safely out of the way, in the cockpit."

THE HORIZON

Once there was a young boy whose father went away and whose mother worked. They lived in one of those dull suburbs where nothing ever happened. His mother would come home from work nearly three hours after he came home from school. He'd finished his homework by then, and was usually watching TV. He was always hungry.

She was always tired when she came home, so she'd order pizza or bring home fish and chips or something after work. He liked the tastes of these foods, so after he was no longer hungry and his mother had enough he'd just keep eating until it was all gone. He always hated sport, so after a while he became quite round.

He didn't make friends easily because he was no good at sport and too good at his lessons, so he basically got through recess and lunchtime as best he could, then came straight back home after school, did his homework, and turned on the TV to wait for his mother and for dinner.

One day he was restless. It wasn't a feeling he was used to. He stretched his arms up. He walked around the living room. He jumped a few times. He still felt restless. For the first time ever, he decided to go for a walk. Just down to the end of the street and back. Just until he settled.

As he walked, he could feel his heart beating, not a feeling he was used to. There was a warm breeze on his cheek. He walked past houses with low fences, and commercial buildings with barriers. A few cars passed, but he seemed to be the only person on foot.

Just before he turned around, the sun was setting. The air was thicker, the light more a red-gold. He fancied he could see a point off in the distance, where there was a line between the thick, orange afternoon light and the green-blue evening light. What would happen if he made it to that line, he wondered.

The next day when he got home from school, he took the two litre bottle of strawberry flavoured milk out of the fridge, drank deeply from the bottle, and put it back in. Then he went down to the garage. His bike would be here somewhere.

It was. It was propped up against the wall, and his mother had leaned a large cardboard box in front of it. In front of that, was the lawnmower. The first thing to do was to was to move the lawnmower. Awkwardly he did that, pushing it to the centre of the garage. Then he needed to move the box, which turned out to be two boxes on top of each other.

He tried to pick up the top one, and found it was heavier than it looked. His fingers could barely hang on and he ached as he walked it, with very small, careful steps, away from his bike. He found that he had to be very slow, lowering it to the ground. The bottom one was a matching box, and was just as heavy and even more difficult to move. He tried lifting it by positioning it between his legs, but he couldn't get a decent grip. Eventually, he just bent over and pushed it along the floor. He resisted the urge to go "brooom brooom brooom" as he did so.

And there was his bike, dusty, and with spider webs on the frame. He pulled it out, and found one of the tyres was completely flat. There was a puncture kit. He took the tyre off as he'd been shown a long time ago, submerged it in a bucket of water, and squeezed. Yes, a line of tiny bubbles came out. Holding the tyre carefully, he picked it up and laid it on the bench and put a loose nail near it so he would remember where the hole was.

Then it was finding and cleaning down a patch, and the glue. It took longer than he thought. When he thought the glue would be dry, he put everything together, got the pump and pumped the tyre up. He hadn't had a lot of practice and it really was very flat, so by the time the tyre was hard his arm was sore. He almost went back inside to watch TV, but he glanced out through the garage door, and the sunlight was just beginning to thicken into that late afternoon gold, so he still had time.

He pushed the bike out onto the street, got onto it and started. It had been ages, and he was a bit wobbly, but after a moment it all came back to him. It was even fun, almost, unless that was just the flush of an achievement, and not real enjoyment at all. He turned off his street, and went down the quieter side-street, towards the back of the warehouses.

And there it was! Once again, he could see the line of twilight, the line shimmering and dancing at the edge of visibility, the line where day and evening turned into each other. He rode as close to it as he could, not taking his eyes off it in case it vanished, and when it was only a metre or two away, got off his bike and threw it down. The line was still there. Carefully, deliberately, he stepped over it, onto it, into it.

The world seemed to wobble a bit. His vision clouded and his eyes felt gritty. He closed them, and rubbed them hard with his fists. When he opened them again, he was standing in an open gateway, tall black poles reaching for the sky. The dirty buildings had gone. He was on a downhill slope, a grey ocean in front of him, with low, choppy waves under a grey sky. There were scattered cottages around, made of aged, silver timber that looked splintery.

He was certainly suddenly a long, long way from home. He took a couple of steps forward, then half-turned, in case he couldn't get back. The gate was still there, tall and forbidding, but beyond it he couldn't see the street near home. He thought that was probably okay–after all, he couldn't see this place when he was on the home side. As long as he could find the gate, that was the important thing.

He started walking. There were two people on the beach fishing, with old-fashioned timber poles and string. There were people coming and going amongst the buildings. They were dressed peculiarly. They all had shirts, men and women, to the knees, and below that, leggings to their pointy boots. They wore all colours, greens and greys and blues … but all the colours were muted, as if overlaid with grey. In fact everything, he realised, was overlaid with grey. It was as if he was wearing grey-tinted sunglasses.

There were two buildings next to each other, both having chimneys with smoke coming out of them. One smelled of burning coal, the other smelled deliciously of some kind of baked food. Bread? Scones? Cakes? He headed towards the two buildings. Before he reached them, a plump woman came out of the bakery, if that was what it was, carrying a basket. She stopped suddenly and squinted, looking right at him, then stood absolutely still with her eyes fixed on him.

With nothing better to do, he walked towards her. "Er, hi."

"Hello, Alien," she said.

He bristled a bit. "I'm not an alien."

"You came through the Gates."

He thought about it. He did come through the gate. She was right—on this side of the gate, he probably was the alien. "I'm sorry. My name is George."

"You are all called Alien. We do not speak your own names for yourself."

"Other people have been here before me?"

"Yes, and others will come again. Not all of them look like you. You're a fine, solid one. Are you hungry after your journey?"

"I'm a bit thirsty."

"Wait here. I need to take this across, then I'll get you something."

He stood as she entered the other building. A wave of heat came from the door as she passed through, then he could hear her voice and a gruff male voice, talking and laughing. After a moment she came back out, her face flushed red and with beads of sweat around the edges of her hairline sticking some of her loose hairs to her skin.

"What happens in there?"

"It used to be the blacksmithy. They used to make tools and all manner of metal objects. Now, because the end of the world is coming, they are unmaking metal things, melting them back down into lumps of metal."

"The end of the world?"

"We always thought aliens would be smarter, but so far none of you have known the world is ending. Cannot you see how grey everything is? In order to die with clear consciences, we need to get rid of everything we own."

She handed him a turned wooden tumbler with a clear liquid in it. He tasted it. It had no taste, but it was somehow richer, thicker than water. And very satisfying. He drank it back quickly. "So is everyone getting rid of stuff?"

"Yes, everyone."

"Even things like jewellery?"

"Most of us are burying or dropping valuables in the ocean and letting the tide take it. One day, the tide will take our bones, too, so it's quite okay."

"Are there any children?"

"There are a few. Nobody's been taking the risk of having children since we found out, but my sister had just become pregnant at that stage, and had the baby girl fifteen days ago. It's all terribly sad, that my niece has not been born in time to have some kind of life, but will die with the rest of us as a little baby. Do you have children, Alien?"

"No." It felt strange to be asked. He was a great big lump of an unloved schoolkid, and she presumed he was a mature man, who might have a child. Was it a compliment, or was she just completely stupid? He didn't think she was stupid.

They had been talking. Now they were down at the edge of the water. His nostrils widened at the smell of the salt and decaying seaweed around the poles of the jetty. Even close-up, the water looked grey, and the sand at their feet was a lighter shade of grey. The fisherman closest to them was packing up.

George looked at him. "What has he thrown out? Looks like he caught a couple of fish instead."

"He's thrown out most of his stuff. He's just catching enough to feed himself and a couple of his neighbours until the end."

"Do you know when the end is coming?"

"They say the sky will turn orange and the sea will evaporate, and we will all burn. We don't know when. Could be today, could be in a few weeks. But it is coming. You should go back to your own world before that. There is a whole life you will miss, and loved ones who will miss you."

George wasn't sure whether his mother world miss him. She'd cry, and bury him, then continue doing whatever it was she did. She's just have more space in the house. And he had no friends, so other people would miss him even less. He felt a terrible wave of loneliness. This woman expected everyone to be loved—he felt the vacuum of love in his life as a sudden, intense ache that he'd never had before.

"I think I need to get home," he said. "My mum will be home from work soon, and I need to be there."

Very well," she replied, "I'll walk you to the Gates."

When they reached it, he looked at her. "Can I talk to you again next time I come?"

"If the world hasn't ended, yes. I'd like that, Alien."

"How will I know if the world has ended?"

"If it hasn't ended, you'll be able to find your side of the Gates in your world where you found it this time. If it's ended, you'll never find it again."

She touched her finger to his forehead in farewell. He smiled, and stepped back through.

The air wobbled and his vision went fuzzy and gritty again. Again, he had to rub his eyes hard to remove the grit. There was the familiar street in the gloaming, and his bike on the ground near him. He picked it up. It didn't have lights and he was wearing dark clothes—he took extra care on the ride home.

He had just propped the bike up against the garage wall when his mother drove in. She smiled at him.

"Been for a ride," she said, surprised.

"Yeah, I thought I would. I was bored. The tyre was flat, I had to fix it first so I didn't go far. I might go again tomorrow."

"That might be just what you need. I brought back hamburgers and chips for dinner, yours is the one with bacon and egg. Let's eat. Then I'll have a shower, and an early night. Work was tough today. You can watch TV until ten, then off to bed, okay?"

"Okay, Mum." He watched TV until ten, then went to bed and played on his mobile until midnight. He was ready to sleep then, but the girl's face and voice kept coming into his mind. Surely their world couldn't be ending.

The next day he woke up stale, and school was even more of an ordeal than usual. Not a single soul spoke to him, but that was really a blessing, because usually they teased him. Still, it underlined what she had made him notice, that there wasn't anybody to care about him. Perhaps, if he visited often, she would care about him.

After school, he went into his mother's room. In her chest of drawers there was the drawer she kept her scarves in. He knew she had lovely scarves: some of them of colourful wool for winter warmth, some of them of colourful silk just for decoration. She hadn't actually worn any of her scarves for ages.

Carefully he pulled them out, one by one, piling them up in order so that when he replaced them they'd be in the same order. About two-thirds of the drawer was cleared before he found the one he remembered: a beautiful translucent one, in turquoise and mauve, with gold thread through it. It was stunningly beautiful. It needed to be worn. That girl would love it. He folded it up small and stuffed it in his pocket.

Then he pulled the bike out and rode to the same place. Found that shimmering line, and stepped through it. He found himself in the gateway again, and again his eyes were crusty and in desperate need of a rub. He couldn't see the girl at all. He walked up to the bakery, and knocked on the door. Then waited. Nothing happened.

"Hello?" He called once or twice, then opened the door and walked in. The girl was there, sweeping up. The fires were off. There were a few rolls and some small loaves on a shelf.

"Nice to see you again, Alien," she said. "The time draws close. I only baked enough for my neighbours."

"I don't want food. I brought you a present."

"A present?"

"This," he said, pulling it out of his pocket. I thought you might like it." I thought you might like it, and I thought it might make you like me.

She held it up. "It's very fine," she said doubtfully. "Full of pretty alien colours and good workmanship that you don't find on this planet. Why are you giving it to me, Alien?"

He felt humiliated, and repeated himself. "I thought you might like it."

"I like it. But I could never wear it, it's too strange. And giving it to me now, when the world is going to end? I'd have to get rid of it to stay free of any connection. Take it away, Alien. Give it to your lover on your own world."

She put it in his hands, obviously fighting tears. He took it, confused. What just happened? Smarting, he walked out without a word and went back up to the gateway. He barely felt the sting as he stepped through it again, and he cycled back home in a daze. He turned on the TV and sat there, numb, until his mother got home.

The next afternoon he went back to the horizon. Through a painful night and a painful day, he had thought about the woman and the scarf. He wanted to make things right with her. And, perhaps, pick up the scarf where he'd dropped it on her side of the gate, and sneak it back into his mother's drawer.

He positioned himself, and waited. And kept waiting. The light changed, but that line between one world and another never came. Half a dozen times he tried to step into it even though he could see nothing, and each time he remained in his own world. Great fat tears rolled over his fat cheeks and dropped on his school uniform.

Every day for weeks he went down there. He could never get across to the other community. He knew now. He loved her. Loved someone for the first time, and lost her immediately as her world ended.

THE SOLDIER'S STORY

Let's just imagine, for the sake of argument, that I'm a soldier. Before that, I was a schoolboy, a schoolboy with an older sister. Our parents had a lot of bad luck over the years, and lost two businesses, and we ended up on the breadline when my sister and I were in high school.

We both hated being poor. She hated not having nice clothes and nice technology. I hated not having the best BMX and the best technology. The difference between us was, it made me miserable, but it made her angry. I remember a lot of shouting and slammed doors in the family home, which was a series of shabby rentals. I didn't slam any of them. I sulked in my bedroom, mostly.

While I spent my high school years sinking deeper and deeper into a torpor, she spent the same time fighting. And not just screaming at our folks, but being hyper-competitive at school, doing exams and track-and-field like she'd die if she came second. She got harder and harder, and stronger and stronger, and smarter and smarter.

When we were little I couldn't compete because she was bigger. As a teen I couldn't compete because she was driven and I wasn't. So I didn't try at all. When we were evicted from one rental and moved to another, it was a long way from our high school, so the two of us transferred over to a different school. There were all the usual problems: having no friends, and not knowing where all the classrooms were, and not knowing where to go, but we managed.

I spent most of my lunchtimes striding around the playground like I was a steroid-hopped teacher on playground duty, while she soon found a bunch of friends. One of those friends was cool and super-attractive, so I kept well away from her, even when she visited us at home. And it turned out that her mother was the careers adviser.

Sis was in and out of their house all the time, and the careers adviser was Mrs Ustinov at school and Peta at home. I wasn't real comfortable with any of this, and I kept my head down. But my sister loved it, and when she was in Year Ten she went to Mrs Ustinov's office and told her that she wanted to get a degree without a HECS debt, and how did she do that? Mrs Ustinov said she didn't know, but she'd find out.

One Saturday I was hanging at home watching TV when Mrs Ustinov came to the house. She asked for my sister, so I rang her. She came racing back from wherever she was, and tore into the house noisily. Called her Peta the whole time, which was just wrong. Turns out, she'd found a way for sis to get a debt-free degree. She needed to get accepted into the Australian Defence Force Academy, ADFA, and do the officer training programme. She needed a certain level of physical fitness and a given ATAR. She'd need to keep going to the intake office regularly during the next two years for physical and psychological testing. If she passed all of that, she'd be in.

So that's what my sister did. Slaved her guts out to end up with a guaranteed job—or a life signed away to slave labour in the military—and a degree paid-for by serving a minimum time in that job. And a proper wage while she studied. She was ecstatic. I thought it sounded dreadful. She worked hard on improving her swimming, which was the only area where she didn't excel, kept her grades up, kept her fitness up, and trotted off for her psych and physical testing every so often. Then it was waiting for the results of the HSC, and she did better than she needed.

She packed her bags and moved to Canberra to study at Duntroon, and I plugged along a couple of years behind her with no such plans, just barely keeping my head out of water. Every so often Mrs Ustinov would call me into her office, and ask me if I'd decided to follow her example, saying she knew I could do it if I tried. I kept saying no. One day I found a garbage bin near the door of the school library full of shredded paperwork. It looked flammable to me, and I was suddenly tempted. I had a cigarette lighter in my pocket—I always did—so I took some of the stuff out of the bin, lit up the stuff in the bin, and put the rest back on top of the flames.

It flared up better than my best expectations. I kicked the bin over into the doorway and walked away. I didn't look back, but I could smell the sharp, chemical smell of the synthetic carpet starting to either burn or melt. For the first time in my life, I felt powerful. I kept walking.

I was young and stupid. I didn't even think about things like security cameras. At the end of the day I was hauled into the Principal's office, and my mother and the police were called. They kept asking me why. How could I explain? That I was bottom of the food chain, that I had no power, that it made me feel powerful? That was true, but sounded so wrong in my head. I said nothing. When my mother promised to pay for new carpet I was let off with a warning, and got screamed at in the car all the way home. My sister, the Golden Child, never even mentioned it to this very day, which was a small mercy. I was dreading her potential cruelty.

Somehow I got through high school. My sister came home for weekends occasionally, but never really spoke to me about anything important. Mrs Ustinov kept quizzing me about what I wanted to do after school, but I didn't want to do anything. All I wanted to do was to melt into the ground and disappear. My best mate started shoplifting seriously, not like a kid but in an organised way. He got me to come to small shops with him and talk to the staff until he grabbed what he wanted and walked out, then I'd leave a bit after him. He stole stuff he wanted and stuff he knew he could sell to friends, and he used to pay me in stolen goods. The only future I could see for myself was unemployment, or petty crime.

After I sat the HSC but before the results came in, my father sat me down and talked to me. He told me for the first time that he loved me, and it broke his heart to watch me frittering my life away. He asked me to promise to try and get at least some kind of honest work. He told me he didn't expect me to be like my sister because we were very different people, but he loved me as much and hoped I'd have a good life in the future, but that it had to start now.

That surprised me a little, I wasn't expecting that at all. It had never occurred to me that he had any particular feelings about me, or that I even could disappoint him. I was watching TV, and an ad came on about army recruiting, one of those flash ads for enlisted people, not officers, where they tell you that you can travel the world and do anything you want to do.

Even I wasn't that much of a fool—I knew it would be harder than that. But I figured I'd have a roof over my head and money in my pocket and I wouldn't have to make any decisions, so it seemed like a pretty good option. I applied. I had to do the beep test and swim a certain distance, and answer a lot of multiple choice questions. At the end, they told me my results were borderline, but they took me anyway.

A few weeks later I was packing a suitcase to leave for basic training, with much less fanfare and glory than my sister left for officer training. It wasn't easy. I had to march for hours with an intolerably heavy backpack in all kinds of dreadful weather. We had minimum sleeping time, so I cut my showers right down just to have a few minutes extra in bed, and even that they randomly broke, entering our dorms with sirens and screamed orders, to simulate combat conditions.

There was a lot I didn't like. The worst was a prisoner of war training exercise. We had to line up in two facing rows, play-acting being both the soldier and the prisoner. We took turns to mace each other in the face, then hold the victim's head underwater. It was bad enough watching the faces of our mates blistering, then having to hold them underwater until we were permitted to release them, nearly drowning them, but then it was our turn to be the victim, once they recovered enough.

The mace was evil. It didn't come out in a mist like police mace sprays, but in a single fine, intense jet which cut right through the skin and felt like the end of the world. Then someone would grab you by the neck and force your head underwater. You could feel some of the mace float off your skin while you were underwater, but the burning of the skin didn't cool down enough. Then when they dragged your head out of the water again, all the mace was floating on the surface of the water, and it slid back on your face again, but not just on the open wound that the jet had cut into your skin, but everywhere.

And it got into your nostrils and lips and eyes as well, even though I had my eyes screwed up tightly. Somebody threw a towel into my hands and I tried desperately to scrub the mace off with the dry towel, but only succeeded in rubbing it into my skin even more. It took days to get my sight back properly, even with an army doctor's efforts, and weeks for the skin burns to subside.

And that, folks, is Basic Training in the magnificent Aussie Army. My sister loved being an officer. I hated being an enlisted man. After the mace session, I took nearly all of my pay out of my bank account every fortnight, and bought myself a vest with secret pockets so I could wear all my money below my uniform.

This is only a story, but if it was true, I'd have kept pulling money out for a few months until I had quite a lot of it, enough for anonymous travel and a new start, then walk off-base without signing out. And get on a train, paying cash. And get on a coach, paying cash. I can't go anywhere I'm known, and I can't use my bank account which is nearly empty anyway, because the military police will find me. But if I was on the run, I'd be looking to find a friendly, rural community that could take on a fit young guy prepared to do manual work for cash and accommodation.

And here I am, in a friendly rural community. I don't suppose anyone around here can use me?

BIOGRAPHY OF A HOUSE

Once, quite a long time ago, in a town called Morningside, an old man died. He had outlived his wife and one of his children, but he still had another four children left. Sixty years earlier, freshly trained as a carpenter and even more freshly in love, he selected a site halfway up a hill in Morningside, and quietly started digging out foundations in the evenings after work and the weekends. He dug out many small holes rather than one big hole, and when he had them dug out, he scoured the block for broken stones, and building sites he was working on for broken bricks.

Then, with a little cement hand-mixed in a bucket, he would jigsaw-puzzle the stones together in the holes, to make footings. He was guided by string strung from posts driven into the ground near the footings, checked with his spirit level, to make sure the footings were all the same relative height, because the land was not flat.

After that he laid fresh floorboards north-to-south, milled from the trees he had cut down to clear the site. Then another layer, east-to-west, and a third, north-to-south. When he was happy with the floor, he threw up a simple timber frame and some walls, beam by beam, partly made from timber from his land, but there wasn't enough, so he bought timber in as well.

He would work all day for his boss, then work a few hours in the afternoon on his house, just waiting to take his girl to the movies or out for dinner sometimes, then sleep deeply until it was time to work again. On the weekends, he'd get up early and build for six hours, then take his girl out in the afternoons. Sometimes he took her to the site to show her the progress.

It took him a year to build the house, even though it was quite a simple house. When it was ready he started building tables and chairs, bed-frames with drawers under them, cupboards and open shelving, all the things a house needs. Some of them were built inside the house, and were too chunky to get out of the doors so would have to stay there forever, but they were lovingly crafted, and nobody would ever want to get rid of them.

When the house was ready he proposed to his girl, and she said yes. They bought things for the house: blankets, curtains, pots, plates. After the wedding they moved in. Five children were born there, one child died there. One by one, the children grew up, learnt a trade, married and moved out. Not one of them became a carpenter.

Thirty-two years passed by in the wink of an eye, or so it seemed to the old man. His wife seemed even lovelier to him now than she had back then, but she became sick. The children visited, to hold her hand and complain about their own children. The old woman died. The children visited, to bury her and bicker over her belongings.

The old man lived alone in his large but simple house, a house built for a family. He still had all his hand carpentry tools. One day he was given many red cedar boards, by a builder who had over-bought. It was very fine cedar: rich and dark, and still smelling divine from having been milled.

He decided to make one last thing: a table. A huge, oval dining table that could seat all of them and all their children, too. A table with ornate hand-carved legs, and ten chairs with matching legs out of the same timber. He would make it inside the house, because it would be too big to get through doorways. It would be the last thing he crafted, his swansong. He would do the most perfect, careful job. It would be his last gift to his children.

It took him months. He used his old-fashioned hand tools for everything. The effort, his sweat, became a part of the gift. Underneath the tabletop, he carved the words "For my children" in perfect copperplate, knowing that the finished table would be far too heavy to turn over, so nobody would ever see those words. When the table was finally assembled, he sanded it by hand many times, with many different grades of sandpaper, ending up after the finest grade using first rough cloth, then the softest cloth he could find, and rubbing it down for weeks to create a satin finish.

When the table was finished, he asked his children to all visit on the same day, with their families. He planned to go to the butcher and buy some fresh meat, and to the baker and buy a big loaf of bread, and the woman next door and buy a basket of vegetables, then pour wine for his children and give food to his children on the magnificent table he had made for them. He would not mention the table—it would just be there.

It never happened. Sometimes one or another of his children came, with or without their family, and they never mentioned the table. But he could never get the whole family around it, and every time he walked into that room and looked at it, and at all the love that went into it, the tears rolled down his withered cheeks.

One day, the old man got sick. Two days he spent in bed, staggering to the tap for a glass of water only when he really had to. One the morning of the third day, he woke to find Death standing at the foot of his bed. "Come with me, old man," said Death, not unkindly. "It's time."

"Wait," said the old man, and struggled to his feet, his blanket wrapped around him. He stumbled to the great family table. Twice he tried to climb onto the table, but he was too weak. "Help me?"

"I'm not really suppose... oh, all right," said Death, giving in and breaking the rules, and gave him a hand. The old man lay down, covering himself with the blanket.

"Are you settled now?" Death asked. For answer, the old man gave a slight smile and closed his eyes. Death made a simple gesture with her left hand, and left the house. The old man's body grew cold.

It took several more days for the neighbour to investigate, and to call the family. The children sat around the table for the first time to plan his funeral. They made a decision not to sell the house and split the money— they chose to keep the house, and rent it out. But first they had to get rid of all the heavier furniture. They sawed up beds, benches, and eventually the dining table. Board by board they threw out the door into a skip bin, never noticing the inscription "For my children" on the underside of the table.

A young couple with dogs rented it first. They had hardly any furniture of their own, and bought shabby stuff from a charity shop. They would have loved the old man's furniture. They both lost their jobs in the same month, and decided to travel. They gave their dogs away, threw out their shabby furniture, and left Morningside.

Next, a middle-aged couple with teenagers moved in. After living there a year and enjoying the house, they talked to the old man's children then to their bank, and bought the place. Their children grew up and moved out, the second old man to live there divorced her, and after he left the old lady lived there until she was too old to look after herself or the house any more. As she aged and before she was forced into care, her grandchildren and all their schoolfriends filled the place with laughter.

After she was gone a young woman who wasn't from Morningside bought the house for her mother to live in. The house and the mother just loved each other, and sang to each other. But the mother was mischievous. By now, the simple house had been expanded, with a large wooden deck out the back. There were bricks from the ground to the deck—it was impossible to see what was under there, unless you got into the crawl-space below the house and deck.

An electrician doing some rewiring for the mother found a wedding ring that had fallen between the boards of the deck. It was the first old man's, that he carefully dropped in there after his wife died, but nobody knew that all these years later. It gave the mother an idea. She went and bought a life-size plastic Halloween skeleton and the next time she had an odd job man in to do some work, she asked him to take it and lay it under the decking in the crawl-space.

It pleased the mother to think that at some time in the future, when she was long gone, those timbers of the deck would need replacing. And someone would pull them up to reveal a skeleton covered in decades of cobwebs and mouse droppings, looking organic and authentic. And that a forensic team would have to investigate before it was revealed it was plastic. This amused the mother very much.

Morningside, an old woman died. Taking her secret joke with her.

SIXTEEN

I might just be a broken-down old woman waiting to die now, but once I was very beautiful. And before I ever became beautiful, which happened when I developed poise, I was very young, and like all young people, awkward. I felt like the ugliest little thing.

I remember looking at him when we were in Year Ten, just a bunch of giggling schoolgirls sitting under the camphor tree near the girls' toilets, smoking our forbidden cigarettes and enjoying them all the better for the ban. We used to roll our school tunics all the way up to our underpants—some of us tucked them into the legs of our underpants—and sit on the sparse grass getting a tan on our legs.

Sue-Marie was the beauty amongst us. She had blue-black hair that we had all taken turns dying for her, a golden, pimple-free skin, a smile that would have put a toothpaste commercial to shame, and rich parents. She was the one that wore designer jeans, antique lace blouses and four hundred dollar leather riding boots to school on Freedom From Uniform Day. She was the one the rest of us tried to be.

Richie was the one we all wanted. While all the rest of them were just pimply boys that none of us would even look at, Richie was a real man. He had been captain of the cricket team of the school all season, and when the district team was picked for the big competition he was chosen as captain of that team as well. In his cricket whites, his well-defined thigh muscles were even more obvious than ever. Everybody used to hush whenever he walked past.

Sue-Marie had been his girlfriend. They looked achingly good together, the beautiful with the handsome. The romance ended, though, with neither of them saying very much about why it ended. If quizzed, Sue-Marie used to say: "Well, you know what they say about younger men. It couldn't have lasted." She was born in July, and he in September.

Now she sat smoking the communal cigarette with us, watching him with eyes narrowed whilst the rest of us watched him with pupils dilated. "Isn't he handsome," Janet said longingly. We all agreed, sighing or in silence. Sue-Marie looked sardonic, but kept her thoughts to herself.

I had never had a boyfriend. I was underweight, the ultimate skinny kid. Underweight might look all right when you are a fully developed woman and have some shape, but I just looked like a sack of bones, all sharp edges and points. And just like any fully developed but underweight woman, I was always tired. I never had any energy, and never really wanted to have any. This business of sitting around lazily and smoking suited me fine. I felt no desire to join the school's tennis club.

During the hot summers I sometimes used to stop at a shop on the way home from school and buy myself an iceblock. I would suck at it until my mouth felt frozen, then throw it away and walk the rest of the way home. Sue-Marie usually got walked home by some lucky boy or other, but I never got walked home at all. Sue-Marie had curves where I had edges.

This day I stopped to buy myself an iceblock. It was raspberry, and runny on this hot day. Raspberry stains awfully, but I thought who's to notice? My fingers turned red. I threw most of it away as usual, and caught a glimpse of myself in the mirrored wall as I left. Red down to my chin and up to my nostrils. Oh well.

There was a group of boys walking home along the other side of the street. Richie was amongst them. He was talking animatedly so he probably wouldn't notice anything, but I turned away anyway so that he wouldn't notice the stains. He seemed to say something to the others, and left the group. He crossed the road. I could have died a thousand deaths—it became obvious he was coming my way. I cringed and kept walking. Perhaps if I didn't notice him he'd change his mind.

As I turned into my own street he caught up with me and tapped me lightly on the shoulder. I felt my stomach flip, and my legs turn to jelly and start to dissolve into the earth.

"Hello Butterfly," he said softly. "I've noticed you at school. What's your name?"

"Nina," I told him, in pain because we were talking when I didn't look my best and because he was seeing me covered in iceblock stains just like a little girl. My voice was little more than a whisper.

"Nina," he said, testing it. "It's not beautiful enough for you. I think I will call you Butterfly."

"As you please," I replied, still dying a thousand deaths. All I wanted to do was to sink into the ground. He must be making fun of me.

Then the unthinkable happened. "Would you come out with me on Friday night, Butterfly?" he asked. "We could borrow my dad's car and go to see Bedazzled at the drive-in. You'll like Bedazzled." He was starting to gabble, but I never for a moment thought he could be nervous. He was the cricket star, and I was nothing.

"Yes," I choked, and bolted for home, alarmed at what I had done.

"Mum!" I screamed as I flew into the house. "Mum! Richie asked me out!"

"Who?" She asked, emerging from the kitchen wiping soapsuds from her elbows. "Who asked you out?"

"Richie. You know, Richie Black!"

"That nice cricketer boy?" she asked, beaming. "What did you say to him?"

I couldn't believe how calmly she was taking it. I wanted to slap her, beat her head against a wall, anything that would make her realise the enormity of the situation.

"I told him I'd go," I whimpered, hanging my head.

"Excellent!" Mum was talking a little too loudly. "You can wear that red party dress you bought." The red party dress would have looked stunning on someone with tits, but on me it just exposed acres of bone with pallid skin drawn tightly across it. I was too young to know this, though, and I thought it looked as stunning on me as on the mannequin in the shop window.

I needed to go shopping. The first stop was the chemist's. I bought every pimple preparation I'd ever seen advertising for, in the hope that I could control my erratic skin in the few days left before Friday. If there had been a tube labelled Poxoff I probably would have bought that as well.

Then I went to the cosmetics stand at Woolworths. I wanted a red lipstick to match the dress, and some dark eye makeup. I spent all the money I had left on a flame-red scarf.

Friday came. My pimples were still there, but my skin was parched between them. The day at school lasted forever. Every time I saw him at school I quickly averted my eyes, and he did not come over. Perhaps he had forgotten our date.

I went home, and soaked in a bath as hot as I could stand. When the water got chilly, I lifted myself out of it. I pulled the crimps out of my straggly, teenaged hair. I put on my nicest knickers, wishing to God I had some silk or lacy ones. I pulled on the red dress. I put heavy gashes of red on my mouth. I lined my eyes heavily with the dark-blue eyeliner I had bought cheap. I scraped some black (I believe they called it "smoke") eyeshadow over my top eyelids. Viewing the results critically in the mirror, I was satisfied with the amateurish results. My mother diplomatically said nothing.

I waited in agony in case he came, and I waited in agony in case he didn't come. If he turned up, I'd somehow have to go through with the evening. If he didn't turn up, what would I say to Mum? I sat in my room.

Eventually the doorbell rang. "Goodbye, Mum!" I called, and flew out of the house before she could bestow any advice on me. There he was, just as he said, with his Dad's Kombi, in his best tailored casual jeans and a loudly striped shirt, his hair still wet from washing. He probably just looked like a nervous teenage kid, but to me he looked gorgeous.

He groped for my hand when we walked down the drive to the car. I had practised holding hands by clasping my hands together, but it felt really strange to hold a hand that was a lot bigger than mine for the very first time. We drove almost in silence to the drive-in, he paid, and he bought me an ice cream before the show. I was starting to think he was nervous. We watched some advertisements, both of us pretending to be interested in the screen.

Then he looked at me. I kept looking straight ahead. "Are you enjoying yourself, Butterfly?" he asked softly. "Because I'm enjoying being here with you."

I said nothing. He tried again. He kept on saying sweet things, then he said that it would be ages before the show. If I was cold he had a blanket in the back and we could see just as well from the back where it was more comfortable.

I resisted. I said I was quite comfortable. I felt as though I was treading on very thin ice. I desperately wanted him to make love to me, but I was terrified. Half an hour into the film the temperature dropped noticeably.

The red dress was made of very thin stuff, and I got cold. So we moved into the back seat.

He fussed around me, ostensibly tucking the blanket around me, stroking me with feather-light touches as he did so. "I like you, Butterfly," he whispered.

"I like you, too," I replied drowsily. I felt much more comfortable with him now. He smiled and continued stroking my arm. I decided I wanted it to happen, and made an abortive movement towards him. He sat up and kissed me clumsily, with too much force. Without a word spoken he lifted my skirt, dragged down my knickers and unzipped his jeans.

"Wait," I said suddenly. I'm not - "

"It's okay," he soothed, taking a condom out of his shirt pocket. "You'll be all right." I quieted down again. I felt as though I was in some sort of trance.

He reached out and put my hand on his limp but rapidly expanding penis. "How do you like that?" he said to me, very proudly.

His pride stung me. I came out of my trance. "Smoked and sliced on rye, with capers and red onion," I snapped.

And watched his erection die, along with my only chance of a romance with the most desired boy in school.

THE WEATHER GODS

Once upon a time, a guy got bored with his job. He used to sit at his deck in the office, and instead of looking at his screen, or at the paperwork in his in-tray, or at the faces of his colleagues at the water-cooler, he just sat at his deck, staring out the window at the little square of sky that he could see from there.

At lunchtime he'd race out of the building, eager to feel the weather on his skin. It didn't matter if it was aching summer heat, or a freezing winter wind, or heavy rain, or even hail, hurling itself down towards him. He just wanted to feel it all, to experience it all.

His lunch-break fell in that twelve-to-one-thirty window that most office workers' lunch-breaks also fell in, so when he was out experiencing the weather in all its forms at the bottom of the deep, concrete canyons that made up the city, all sorts of other people would be out, too. Most of them would be rushing to their favourite lunch retailers, then back to their office or to the city parks. A few would be meeting people in inner city pubs for lunch, as an excuse to get slightly drunk before facing the afternoon's work.

He just walked. And walked, and walked.

After a couple of years, he developed a route through the city, that started and ended at his office, without any doubling back, and lasted about as long, to walk, as his lunch-break was. After he walked it a number of times, he started noticing other people who were also creatures of habit.

There was the woman with the red stiletto ankle-boots. She wore power-suits in a variety of solid colours, but summer and winter, she always wore the same boots. He could hear her click-clicking from a distance, through the other street sounds.

There was the guy with the corroding nose. It was un-hidden by any form of mask or makeup. When he started noticing him, it was grotesquely swollen and misshapen, and bright pink to red. Over two years of seeing him five days a week, it gradually ate itself up, developing ulcers, then holes in the tissue, until the nose was one black-and-red hole in his face, with him seeming unaware of it and still making no effort to hide it. His face was always clean-shaven—our hero always wondered how he faced himself in the mirror each morning.

Every day he walked. At home, he became more and more abstracted, thinking about the weather, and constantly flicking to news channels when his wife was trying to watch something else, or to the weather app on his phone when there was no weather being broadcast on TV. Weather fascinated him. People seemed less important.

One day when he was walking through the crowd at lunchtime, he saw the Goddess of the Rain. It could only have been her. She was slender and damp, wearing a straight grey skirt and a white puffy top, just like virga falling from a cloud. She seemed to have a fine mist around her, just around her, not around the people surrounding her. People seemed instinctively to part to let her through, not something city crowds ever did for anyone.

He chased after her, not knowing how to call her. She turned a corner, and he ran to the corner. She had vanished utterly. He continued his normal route, but couldn't get her off his mind. There was a rain goddess out there. He knew. He had seen her. Day after day, he lingered near that corner, and never saw her again.

One day, his wife said she was going to divorce him.

"Why," he asked, bewildered.

"You don't even know I exist."

"Yes I do."

"Well, I'm in your way, then. Are you in love with somebody else?"

"No," he replied, trying to look honest, but he knew he was. He was in love with the weather. And with the rain-goddess, who was a part of the weather. "If you want a divorce I can't stop you," he went on. "You can have the house. I don't mind where I live, any more."

"Do you plan to move in with your girlfriend, is that it?"

"I don't have a girlfriend."

He left it up to her to progress the divorce. Soon they came to a point where she said he needed to move out. He made enquiries, and a few days later packed his clothes, some personal items, and took down a large canvas in the living room, an oil of a lighthouse between ocean and land, in the middle of a wild storm. He got his wife to do him one last favour: move his bags, a single box and the painting, in her little car from their house in the suburbs to a room above one of the city pubs, quite close to work.

The room had a queen-sized bed with worn-out but clean bedlinen, an ensuite, and a television. It would do for a man on his own. He hung his work suits and his jeans in the wardrobe, and put his folded clothes in the drawers. Then he took down the picture of a vase of flowers from above the bed, hung his storm painting, and took the hotel's picture down to their reception for them to put it away.

Because he was living there long-term, they had negotiated a reasonable rent, and housekeeping came in only once a week, to vacuum, change his sheets and wipe down the bathroom. This happened when he was at work on Thursdays, so he tended to tidy up on Wednesday evenings.

At first he watched television in the evening, but eventually it dawned on him that he didn't have to fit in with other people's expectations. And just as he wandered through the streets of the city at lunchtime, he started wandering at night, too.

A different world was revealed to him. People came and went from the pub two floors below him. It seemed quite noisy, with too-loud music and the smell of beer over endless conversations—thank goodness the sound didn't penetrate upwards, into the rooms. The streets weren't crowded. A few cars cruised around, and a few people, mostly young and mostly in groups, moved around. Our hero became aware that this was his life, now.

One evening he was out, walking under the street lights and past the spills of lights from shop and office windows, under a light mist. It blew diagonally in the warm summer breeze, catching the lights and looking like silver sparkles. The pavement was wet enough to become three-dimensional, with deep slashes of light and colour penetrating it into the depths.

He crossed a road against the lights—and caught a glimpse of the rain-goddess. He ran after her, calling.

"Rain, Rain!"

She glanced around, and hesitated. He caught her up. Close up she seemed ethereal: flesh and blood, but somehow translucent, made of the rain. "They spell my name R-A-Y-N-E," she told him. "Just thought I'd get that straight, right now. What's yours?"

He told her. Then asked "You want to come for a drink with me?"

She half-laughed. "A drink is not what I need. But you could visit me, I suppose. It's just me and the kids, tonight. Their father has gone out."

He would have wondered what kind of a mother leaves their kids alone, but he was completely transfixed by her, by his long-term love of her finally being made real by her presence.

She led him down by the railway line. In among all the sheds and workshops there was a dilapidated little cottage he had never noticed before, with faded lace curtains and a wooden slated roof with weeds growing in it. She opened the door.

A small, sticky child hurled himself at her. He grabbed her, and swung around her. "Hello, Wind," she said lovingly, then picked his hands off her skirt. "We have a guest tonight. This is my son, Wind."

A small girl emerged from the shadows. She looked dishevelled and wore a most impressive sulk on her face. "And this is my daughter, Cloud. Smile for the nice man, Cloud."

"Shan't," said the little girl, pouting.

By the time he got home, our hero was dancing on air. The rain-goddess was called Rayne, and had children called Wind and Cloud. What could be more fitting? And he had an ongoing invitation to drop by any time he liked. And Rayne had kissed him lightly on the lips at the doorstep when they said goodbye–her lips were cool and moist, and tasted a little like fog.

He adored her, but he didn't want to crowd her. He decided he'd go down to the train tracks to see Rayne every Tuesday and Thursday. The rest of the time, he would just daydream about her. The children would rarely leave them alone. Sometimes she would send them outside to play, and at times like these he could relax. He never wanted to force himself on her, though, and she never seemed open to sex: a cool distance that was utterly desirable had developed between them. He was just happy to breathe the same air she breathed.

On days when the kids were sent out to play, she would call them back when he was ready to go back home. They would come back in, Wind like a little human tornado, and Cloud would drift in reluctantly and say she was hungry. When they came inside he would go back out, and find that the weather had turned. It would be blowing quite hard, and the sky would be completely covered with clouds, the lights of the city reflecting on them and showing them up as something more than a starless sky.

One night when it was just the two of them, and her and the kids were out playing, he asked about their father.

"Sunny," she answered. "Suneel, if you like. You'll never see him much this time of day. He takes care of them during the day sometimes when I'm busy, and he is sociable with others only during daylight hours."

"Are you married? Or …"

"Gosh, no, nothing like that. We are … more or less work colleagues. We both have roles to carry out. And of course, we share the children. Each of us contributes to their development in our different ways."

"Can I meet him?"

You probably already have. Look for a cheerful, glowing man, a man everybody likes. Someone with spots on his face. He likes to call them his Sunspots."

"So … if we were to start properly dating, I mean, if you decided you liked me enough, would he be a problem?"

"He doesn't own me. Nobody owns me. You wouldn't own me, if we were dating."

This encouraged our hero. Week after week, he kept going back to the little cottage, to bask in the company of Rayne, the goddess of rain. Week after week, he did even less of his work, and his colleagues became more and more impatient with him. He hardly noticed their criticism, or the fact that they frequently took files out of his in-tray and processed them themselves.

He had acclimatised well to living in a single room in a pub. He barely remembered his former life, with his wife in a house that needed lawns mowing and stuff picked up. Now his life was all about Rayne, and filling the hours between visits.

He realised he was completely obsessed when he checked his weather app, and realised he hadn't checked it for over a month. He was getting his weather from the horse's mouth. He loved visiting a weather goddess, and watching her raise a couple of budding weather gods. He needed to get to know Sunny.

He didn't expect the response he got from her when he asked. She clamped down, texted him a link, and showed him out of the house. She refused to listen to his protests and apologies. When he got home, he looked at the link. It was to a website that tracked solar flares and sunspots.

The following Tuesday, he tried to visit her again. He went down to the tracks, and walked past shed after shed, factory after factory. There was no cottage. Rayne had gone, taking with her Wind and Cloud. His future stretched out before him: nothing but sunshine, drought, heat and pain. He needed mist. He needed precipitation. He needed sleet, hail, and all other manifestations of Rayne. How could he live without her?

And the drought set in. Settled in. Killed crops, emptied dams, cracked the very soil. He could not cry. Without Rayne, he was too parched.

THE GOOSE GIRL

Once upon a time, a king and queen ruled their country fairly and well. They had a daughter, who grew into an attractive teenager. One day the queen got sick, and became sicker and sicker, instead of getting better. The doctors simply didn't know what to do for her.

One day she called the princess into her bedroom. "I'm not sure I'm going to last much longer," she told her. "And your father's not well, either. The king in the next kingdom is single, and he's agreed to marry you. This means you'll have help running this country, and you'll start popping out babies to take your place in the future. Pass me a tissue?"

The princess did. The queen coughed almightily in it, then folded it up tight. "Here, take this," she said, twisting it a little. "It contains a sample of my DNA. If you keep this with you, there'll always be at least a little of me keeping you company."

The princess thought that was a nice idea, and stuck it in her pocket. Back then, big ballgowns always had plenty of pockets.

"Oh, and take my jewellery box, too. There's some nice things in it. If worst comes to worst, you can always pawn some of the collection. Oh, and wear the big emerald brooch when you arrive there. That will be the proof to all of them that you're the right person and not an imposter." So the princess moved the jewellery box from her mother's room to her own room.

In time, her mother died, and her father lost interest in her because of his grief. The last thing he did for his daughter was to arrange a firm wedding date. A week before the wedding, she chose a carriage, and a couple of the finest horses, and packed her bags with the jewellery box and a few nice dresses.

"Can I come?" asked her favourite servant, a girl only a few years older than she was.

"Sure! I won't know anyone there. I'll need a friendly face." And so they set out on the journey to the other kingdom, so that the princess could get married. The princess remembered what her mother said, and carefully wore the big emerald brooch for the trip.

Now, just as the princess had led a sheltered life and had no idea what it felt like to wear jeans and a teeshirt and work for a living, her servant had no idea what it was like to not have to do anything you didn't want to do, and to wear silk all the time. She had been poor all her life, and her family had been poor before her. All that stretched out in front of her, was a lifetime of serving others, and dying without anything to show for all the work. It really didn't seem fair to her. Why should princesses get all the breaks? Why do kings always marry people who are already rich? And it would do the kid good to do some real work, for a change, it would be character-building.

Aloud, she said "Why don't we play a game? We could swap clothes. You could pretend to be my servant, and I could pretend to be a princess, just for a little while." And maybe, she thought to herself, just maybe the king will fall in love with me. If we were equals in society I'd probably be just as worthy of love. I'm a likeable person, yes?

The idea sounded like fun to the princess. She put on the servant's clothes, which felt heavy and stiff. The servant put on her clothes, which felt like wearing mist. The servant gave her a few silly commands, like "give me a sandwich," and "open that jewellery box and put the nicest necklace on me," and the princess complied, saying "yes, ma'am" each time. But she tired of the game. It wasn't fun any more.

On the other hand, the real servant was having extreme fun, pretending to be royalty. "I don't like this any more," said the real princess. "Can we change back?"

"No," said the servant. "You are really my servant now. And I am really a princess, off to marry a king." The new servant cried and begged, but her new mistress was unrelenting.

And it was with their roles reversed that they approached the castle in the neighbouring kingdom's capital city. They pulled up out the front, and were met with a delegation of fine people, who whisked away the new "princess" after checking that she had a big emerald brooch pinned to her dress, while it was left to a servant to show the new servant to the back entrance, where she was welcomed as an equal in the kitchen, and put to work peeling potatoes, when she had never peeled a potato in her life.

She was not a fast learner. Eventually the servants put her out in the yard, to help the yardboy watch the livestock. She groomed her own horses, and shovelled manure, and watched the hens and the geese. It wasn't as much fun as being a princess, but at least she wasn't dead.

What she missed most was having someone to talk to. She couldn't possibly tell any of the servants here what happened—they already pushed her around. She took to spending a lot of time in the stable, talking to her horses. In time, she focussed on only the one, who seemed to be a better listener than the other one.

Word got back to the new queen - the marriage had happened, now - that her servant talked to animals, and she came out to have a look. Just as they said, she was in the stable, telling her horse how hard it was that her servant had taken over her rightful place in life.

The new queen didn't like hearing that kind of talk, and needed to put a stop to it before anyone else heard. She didn't think giving orders to kill a servant would go down too well, so she told the castle's butcher that she had a hankering for the taste of horsemeat, and told him which horse to kill.

It was a fine-looking horse, he thought, so the butcher got a friend of his from the city who did taxidermy to stuff it, and he hung it in the servants' quarters. That could have been a mistake. The new girl started talking to the stuffed head, just as she did to the living horse. The butcher, the butler and the head housekeeper all listened for a day or two. The girl spoke with an aristocratic accent. And she bemoaned the day she ever swapped clothes with her servant. She talked about how hard it was to serve a queen whom she knew was really only a commoner.

What a fantasist, they all thought, and that was the end of that. None of them suggested to the king that he had married the wrong girl—the new queen had been wearing fine clothes and the big emerald brooch when they arrived. And she had taken to queening like a natural—all haughty and disregarding the servants. They all lived happily ever after, except the proper princess. And even she found that she quite liked the geese.

COMING OUT

Male ego being what it was, we lived in his flat after marrying rather than in my house. I missed my own gardens: in the front, tall tropical rainforest timbers from North Queensland adapted beautifully to cooler southern climes, growing close together over dark, mysterious coolnesses which were the joy of my life, their canopy creating a trickle of green-filtered light and an umbrella of leaves waterproof against all but the heaviest of deluges. I used to sit out there, reading in the pouring rain, the envy of my neighbours. Out the back there were broken chunks of sandstone and granite, and small flowering things like stunted boronia and bush-roses growing between them, a hot, parched landscape.

I had worked hard on my house before moving. Having fallen in love with the gardens, I bought the house almost sight unseen. All those bedrooms! A single girl didn't need them all. So I took down all the inner doors except the bathroom and the laundry door (which were rooms I always felt needed to be hidden), and hung hippy beaded curtains in all the doorways long before they were fashionable. Not the plastic beads of today, but wooden painted and plain beads, segments of bamboo cane, and most luxurious, mysterious and erotic of all, cowrie shells of graded sizes on the main bedroom doorway.

The smallest bedroom of all shared an inner wall with the living room, so for several days I had workmen in, cutting a huge circle in that shared wall and replastering and repainting it. The bottom of the circle was only just above floor level, making it easy to step from one room to the other, the top and sides of the circle filling the wall nicely. The smallest bedroom suddenly became an alcove, with a soft, quiet energy which was greatly helped by the green light filtering through the rainforest trees standing guard outside the windows. It was here I set up my Altar, my meditation space, and my magical rocking-chair, that I used to use for shape-shifting.

The rest of the house was open space now, the beaded curtains giving an illusion of moving from space to space in the house and adding mystery and beauty without walling anything off. I loved the house when I had finished spending money on it, and I had loved the garden from day one. My one regret was that, in servicing a large mortgage and putting money away to spend on extravagant five-star trips all over the place, I worked sixty-hour weeks doing things I detested, spending less time than I would have liked in a restful, peaceful home.

Things went from bad to worse, and as they did, Jimmy got more and more insistent that I marry him. The more he asked, the more I resisted. I didn't know why—all I knew was that the whole boy-girl thing was fraught for me, that it didn't work, that I was inexplicably unhappy when I should have been ecstatic. He kept saying that perhaps I was nervous, perhaps subconsciously I was afraid of him leaving me. Marriage, he said, would assure me that he wasn't going to shoot through, and I'd relax and be happier.

It seemed like an explanation.

The wedding was horrible. It was dominated by grouchy old women who bullied me, summer heat and sweat, and constricting fairytale clothes. I longed for the comfort of scruffy jeans and a stained but Officially Clean tee-shirt of the ancient variety. The honeymoon was worse: Jimmy took me to his dream Pacific resort, which was even hotter than Brisbane and where it rained the whole time. By the time we came back home I was covered in heat-rashes and mosquito bites. It was actually a relief to rock up to the ghastly corporation where I worked and deal with unpleasant office politics and frustrated clients—in the dry, hard, cold air-conditioning.

I didn't relax. I didn't get happier. The whole idea of him leaving me wasn't the problem. I was twenty-three—I had been with him for two years, and before that, had had two other unsatisfying relationships with men. I was obviously one of these women with unrealistic expectations, someone who would never be happy no matter how much people did for her.

As soon as we came back from the honeymoon Jimmy insisted in moving me into his flat. It was a luxury flat in the leafy riverside suburbs, in a security block with swimming pools, saunas, parklands, manned security ... the lot. He had a spacious flat on the second floor and two lock-up garages in the basement. I had my dream house, a house I couldn't imagine him living in and where he was always uncomfortable visiting. I gave up and moved in. He paid his mortgage, I paid mine. I kept finding excuses every time he mentioned putting tenants in my house–it was my space, my private space, tailored to my needs, and a tenant would only be an intruder, violating my home and my extended body.

Likewise, I felt like a stranger in his flat, but one thing I did enjoy very much at the end of a long, hard, tiring day in the city was to come home, grab a towel, head down to the basement and use the sauna until my heart was racing, my hair was soaked and slightly curly, and I was thirsty enough to burst. As far as I could tell, of the many people who silently and invisibly lived alongside each other in the block, I was the only one who used the sauna.

Then one day, four months after the wedding, I took my towel and went down there as usual. This evening, in the midweek, the red light was on outside and I could hear the clicking of the sauna rocks expanding and contracting. Someone else was using my sauna! I called out, intending to leave if a male voice answered, and asking if I could share the sauna if a female voice answered. The voice was female, and asked me to enter. I stripped, wrapped my towel around me, and pushed the heavy wooden door inwards. In the mellow half-light I saw a young woman sitting on the teak bench, wrapped in her towel. Oh well, I liked sauna-ing naked, but if her comfort-zone was to be wrapped, I'd stay wrapped also.

We got introduced - her name was Theresa. She looked like a Pacific Islander, a short person with midbrown skin, curly shoulder-length black hair, a wide mouth with full lips that had a generous and slightly mischievous smile, and the deepest brown eyes I had ever seen: eyes of intelligence, humour, tenderness and pain. She passed along her rock-salt to scour my skin and help draw out toxins. She passed along her essential oils. The most I'd ever brought down with me previously was my towel and maybe a bottle of drinking water. This was luxury.

She had been there a fair while before I'd arrived, she told me, and she needed to get out. She handed her essential oils to me, and told me what flat she lived in. I smiled, telling her that I and my husband lived directly below her flat, on the second floor. I promised to return her oils. She went away. I steamed myself until my body was about to drop, then had a long shower afterwards. I pulled a comb through my wet hair, threw on my clothes, took her oils, and went upstairs to return them.

I knocked lightly on her door, expecting her to take the oils and my thanks, and close the door on me. Instead, she flung the door open widely, grasped me by both wrists, pulled me in, chattering all the time about whether I liked Chinese tea or not, and whether I was allergic to joss sticks, a form of unperfumed incense.

"I thought you were a Pacific Islander," I remember telling her.

"No, Chinese," she said. "My father was white, so my mother tells me. My Chinese name is Bik-Lin. It means Water-Lily."

I smiled silently. She was too earthy to be a water-lily. I could see her as a field of waving corn ripening under the sun, or as a bush-covered valley. Freshly sauna-ed and showered, she still smelled organically of woman. Sitting there, chatting and drinking cup after cup of steaming Chinese tea, I found I rather liked the smell rising from her warmly. I shivered suddenly.

She was all concern. "Are you cold?' she asked, stroking my bare arm gently. Then suddenly she was sitting on my lap bending down to my face, kissing me deeply. Her arms were wrapped around me, both firmly and tenderly.

"You're straight and she's a woman," my Head said. "This is where you push her off your lap and stand up, acting offended."

"Hey, just a moment," my Body protested in reply. "This feels good. In fact, very good. I think I'll just wait a while and see where it's going before I let you make any rash decisions."

Between the two parts of me I stood independently, flushed and exultant, excited and nervous, aroused and aghast at just how quickly I'd been turned from a wife into a dyke; and suddenly decided that I knew at last exactly why all my relationships with men had failed.

When I returned home that evening, Jimmy was in a panic. Two of his friends were there. I had taken longer than ever before to come back from the sauna, and as my car was still in the garage, they were certain I'd been abducted. When I walked in, the atmosphere changed quickly from one of fear to one of menace. The friends left hastily. I tried to tell Jimmy that I'd only been upstairs with a neighbour who had been using the sauna, but he was only reassured when I mentioned that she was a woman who lived upstairs. "I'm tired," I said when he tried to embrace me, and I went into the bathroom to have my third shower for the day.

Afterwards, I went straight to bed despite the hour, hoping to feign sleep when he would come to join me later. I lay for a long time looking at the texture of the wall, controlling my breathing until after he had settled down and started snoring lightly. I lay there until the first glimmer of pre-dawn light, wondering how to tell a brand-new husband that I loved him dearly but had to get divorced immediately.

It took two months to find the right words, and to realise that I'd never find the right time. When I said the words that I had rehearsed so many times, he was as upset as I'd imagined.

"Is there someone else?"

"Yes."

"It's Ian, isn't it."

"No."

"His brother, then. You flirt with his brother sometimes."

I laughed humourlessly. "Sweetness, I flirt with everyone. It doesn't mean anything. It's not his brother."

"Who, then?"

I hesitated. "Theresa."

Disbelief. Then a deep breath, and: "But she's a woman."

"That'd be right."

"You're leaving me for a *woman*?"

"Yes," almost inaudibly. My throat was closing over–I could hardly speak.

"How can I compete with that?" His right hand balled into a fist. Here goes, I thought. The family tendency to settle issues with violence. I should have known he's no better than his brother.

Then the fist opened into a stiff hand. I stood my ground. I wasn't going to become like him. No matter what, I would take the moral high ground, and not hit back.

Then it closed again. Before I could move, he lunged at me, swerved, and drove his fist through a gyprock wall. Slowly he withdrew it. He had lost a lot of skin, and was bleeding heavily. One of the knuckles didn't seem to be sitting right.

I was appalled. My usual role cut in then, and I automatically said: "Come here—I'll clean that up."

He jerked away from my outstretched hands violently. "You'll not touch me!" he hissed. "How dare you!"

"But you're hurt."

"You should have thought of that before you said what you said."

He left the flat. Through the open windows, I fancied I heard the engine of his bike kick over, then cough as he killed it, aware that he didn't have enough strength in his injured hand to ride properly. Tears stinging in my eyes, I grabbed enough clothes for the following day, a toothbrush and a comb, and went out into the evening, towards my long-vacant house. He was not in the garage when I climbed into my car and drove the twenty minutes to my own place.

Over the next months I tried to cut back my working hours to something resembling a normal working week, but it wasn't easy. After a while, I opted for starting my day before seven instead of nine, and working straight through without a break in order to try and manage to have the late afternoons to myself. If I could leave the office at four, I could get to Jimmy's place before he got home from his work. That gave me a chance to gather a few of my possessions each evening without any unpleasantly weepy scenes. When I finally had all my clothes, books and things at my own place, I left my copy of his keys on the hall shelf, and walked out of there for the last time.

At the same time, Theresa was a source of great delight in my life. She didn't want to leave her flat and I didn't want to leave my house: we were both happy with visiting each other frequently, thinking of ourselves as a couple, and sleeping alone from time to time. As I was ruled by my job and the perceived need to earn huge amounts of money, she was too, by her own job. The difference was, she worked in the travel industry and loved what she did, while I worked in finance and loathed earning a good living through ruining other people's lives.

When we first kissed, she was working as a bottom-of-the-rung office slave in a travel agency that belonged to a large chain. By the time I left my husband, she was managing her own branch. A few months after that, she rang me at work one afternoon.

She named my favourite restaurant, where I was such a regular I always got my pick of tables and could request dishes not shown on the menu. She asked if I'd make a booking for that night. Smiling, I said yes, and told her I was busy, and rang off. I made the booking, then got back into what I had been doing before she called.

That evening I went home, pulled off my business suit, put on something softer and more flattering that she preferred, and went and picked her up. As usual, she had just about managed to pull a comb through her hair, but aside from that was in a sartorial state of chaos and disorder that, while it wasn't technically well-groomed, suited her beautifully. As we drove towards the sea, the sun set and the long orange bands of light merged into pink afterglow. I flipped up my headlights and tore along the coastal road at some speed, happy to be with my love, happy to be dining somewhere I loved, happy just to be driving.

The Maître d' gave me a hug when we arrived, shook Tess' hand, and led us to the best table out on the decking over the sea. It was Autumn, but it was one of those warm, caressing nights when it's a joy to be alive. A waiter came along unbidden with a bottle of white wine, a gift from the boss, and lit the candles on the table. The soft light reached all the way to the dark ripples below our feet.

We ordered some of the most tender chilli mussels I'd ever experienced, and shared a cold seafood platter afterwards. Then the coffee and fifty-year-old port came to the table. I was already light-headed from the wine, and feeling really, really good, if slightly disconnected from my body. Tess leaned back, sipped her port, and looked at me speculatively.

"I've got something to tell you," she began.

"Cough it out," I smiled, feeling her nervousness. "It can't be that bad."

She didn't look reassured. "I've been offered another promotion," she started. "I get to manage a whole region of branches, five of them, starting in two months."

"Congratulations!" I said, really meaning it. "You deserve it!"

"The trouble is," she continued as if I hadn't spoken, "the chain I'm going to be managing is in Perth."

"Oh."

There was a long silence. In that silence, her Mastercard disappeared from the table, and silently reappeared for a signature. She bent her head to sign the docket, and I brought my hand up to my face. I couldn't ask her to give up the perfect job. (Could I?) She wouldn't ask me to throw away everything I'd worked for, so I wouldn't ask her to throw away everything she worked for.

The waiter refilled our coffee cups, and went away again. Unshed tears were hanging just behind my eyelids, and I felt stone-cold sober. The Maître d' came out and asked if everything had been to our satisfaction. I couldn't meet his eyes. "Yes, Danny," I said, and got up from the table clumsily.

At the car as I went to unlock her door, she placed her hand on my wrist, stopping me. "Are you okay about it?" she asked softly.

I didn't meet her eyes. "Yes, of course. It's the perfect job for you. You'll love it." I laughed, a bit too loudly, pulled my hand away, opened her door, and walked around to the driver's side. An hour later I was once again lying on my side next to a person I couldn't touch, listening to them sleep.

The next morning, everything seemed normal. In the following weeks Tess spent some time concentrating on winding up loose ends at work and talking to estate agents about selling her place. I spent my days working my guts out and my evenings gathering the few traces of her in my place into a travel bag for her to take away when the time came. We cuddled a lot and we talked nonstop, but there was a huge hole in our conversation surrounding the subject we should have been talking about most.

Months passed. One day shortly in early Spring I drove her to the airport. She had several large suitcases which would cost her a fortune in excess baggage, but this seemed inadequate when I considered that this was all she now owned in the entire world. It was one of those blowy, icy-rainy Sydney winter days, the sort that make people hate to get out of bed. The wind was so strong that when we were on the freeway out to the airport the side-winds seemed to be trying to push my car into the lane next to me.

I parked, and Theresa found a silver trolley for her bags. We ended up needing two. Stuffed with people, the terminal echoed as if it were hollow and deserted. We checked her luggage in, and I led her to a hideously priced and hideously furnished coffee lounge, where we waited, listening to the flights being called on the P.A. system. After hers had been called twice, Tess dropped some money on the table and we rose. The departure gate wasn't far away, and we stood there, holding each other and kissing and hugging like teenagers going home from a school camp.

The last call was announced, and she kissed me square on the mouth for the first time ever in public. As I reeled from the surprise, she turned and started walking. I waited, watching the short woman with the curly hair disappear through the departure gates, waiting to wave if she cast a look over her shoulder at me. She didn't, and suddenly I knew she was gone forever, that it was all over, that she was going towards something that meant more to her than I ever could—her future. I was only her past, and probably an unimportant part of it.

I lowered my head to hide my eyes, and pushed past a dark-blue double-breasted jacket. "Hey!" a man's voice said, but I kept going. I stumbled and asked directions and stumbled again, until I found the airport bar. A child who looked too young to be drinking never mind selling the stuff, poured me a double brandy into an ice-free tumbler and gave me directions to the outdoor observation deck. Brandy in my left hand, car-keys in my right, I stumbled off in the direction she had indicated, and eventually I found the way.

By the time I got there it seemed as if hours had passed since Theresa hadn't looked back at me. The cold air whipped my face but I didn't care. It couldn't hurt me more than I deserved. A large Lufthansa jet was taxiing into position. Further away, I could see an Australian plane. Was that hers? The Lufthansa started its run. I noticed another Australian plane further away and harder to see. It too was taxiing along. Which one was she in? Or had hers already flown while I was getting the drink and finding my way out here?

I hastily took another mouthful, feeling it burn my bitten lip in contrast to the cold.

"Are you all right, lady?" A Small Person squinted up at me.

I gathered my thoughts. "I'm fine. I'm all right."

"You don't look it." Total disbelief from a child.

"Lucy! Come over here!" Her mother had just noticed that she'd wandered. Funny, as I looked at the mother's face she seemed fearful of me. What was wrong?

Then I heard a heart-wrenching sound—the sound of my own sobs. I should have asked Tess not to take the job. I should have dropped everything, resigned my job, sold up and followed her. I should have dropped to my knees in the middle of the airport, recited Elizabethan love poetry and kissed her hand until she decided she couldn't live without me; because standing on that observation deck I'd just discovered I couldn't live without her. Twenty-four years old, and my life was over. How could I live alone ever again? Just when I discovered the real pattern of my life, I had to lose the only person I'd ever cared for. I silenced myself, turned my back on the child and her mother, devoted myself to my brandy.

What must I have looked like, a young woman drinking alcohol and ugly-crying on the observation deck? When social media became a thing I looked for Theresa, but even before we separated she had changed her surname twice. I figured she changed her name like other people changed their addresses, and I'd never find her. And I never did.

SPIDERS I HAVE KNOWN

I'm getting old now, and I've been alive a long time. In that time, I've met a few spiders, and some were even characters.

There was the bathroom spider, a daddy long legs, a species of spider in the Pholcidae family of spiders, I've forgotten exactly which species. As common as muck throughout most areas of Australia. They are so fragile, with their long incredibly slender and breakable legs. In the twentieth century there was a belief that because they were so frail, the only way they could hunt was by having an incredibly powerful venom, but in the early years of this century that was proved to be false. Their venom was collected and tested, and it's innocuous to humans.

This particular one lived in my bathroom in the late nineteen eighties. At the time I lived in a coastal town back east, and it was reasonably humid. I was renting a dodgy fibro shack at the time, which had probably been someone's beachside holiday house, and as a holiday house it would have been fine. But as a permanent residence, it was just a hole.

One of the things that made it so, were windows which had been nailed shut by a previous resident, so that you could never get any airflow happening. The house was permanently mouldy as a result. Another was that the only plumbing that was plumbed properly was the toilet–all the other drains, in sinks and showers, were just drain-holes with no pipes, so the water dripped on the land. This was probably meant to be a water-saving measure, irrigating the garden without using extra water, but it also meant was that up through the drains came all kinds of small wildlife at night, notably slugs and millipedes.

At some stage a daddy long legs realised this, and set up camp in my bathtub-shower. I was never a fan of baths but I do like a good shower, and at that stage of my life I was showering in the evening. So every night I'd go into my bathroom, where the spider would have built a complex web over the drainhole, with extensions up the wall. I'd brush my teeth, which was the spider's cue to start climbing.

Even with her extensions, it was still an arduous climb for a little creature, especially in the bathtub where the enamel was slipperier than the tiles above, and much slipperier than the painted wall above that. She regularly lost ground, sliding several centimetres back and having to climb that distance a second time. Once I knew that was happening every night, I'd watch and wait before I turned on the shower, so that she was safe. Once I turned on the shower, her higher extensions would be there, but her drainpipe catching-web would be washed away, and she'd rebuild it every day.

Spiders get old a lot faster than humans do. She must have gone down the drain-hole occasionally and come back up having had sex, because every so often I'd see her secure an egg-ball to her web. Then there would be millions of mini-spiders around for a day or two, then they would scatter. Mum stayed around for ages. Then she got old, and one day she was dead in her web.

I flushed her dead body and much of her web down the drain that night. Imagine my surprise twenty-four hours later, then I found it reconstructed, and found a slightly smaller spider of the same species on the web! I'm certain it was one of her children or grandchildren. As I brushed my teeth she had already reconstructed the catching-web over the drain, but as she climbed she was pausing here and there, and seeming to taste the old web she was climbing on.

That fascinated me. Did the taste of the old web confer coded spider-knowledge? It certainly seemed to. Right from day one, she knew to climb up to the ceiling when I was brushing my teeth, and to climb down and start repairing her web when I was drying myself off.

In the same house, I had a side gate that I occasionally used. It had a St Andrews spider hanging there, one of the Argiope species, with its golden belly and its beautiful diagonal cross web. I believe they are part of the larger orb weaver family, but to me, orb weavers are really only musicians—look up the song *The Distant Call of Home*. So poignant.

Anyway, this girl used to hold onto her web and not run away at all when I opened the gate. She knew I wasn't going to harm her, and I knew she was there and moved slowly so as to not cause damage to her web. It would hang loose until I shut the gate again, but was never damaged. She would have babies at regular intervals, too. And a few days after emerging from the egg sac, they would go away. She got older, too, and lost a leg or two with time and mating battles.

When she had her last family, most of them disappeared at the usual time, but a few hung around in her web. Then one day when I checked on them, Mum had gone. There were just the daughter-spiders, and they were having a massive all-in brawl. When I came out a few hours later to check, there was one triumphant one in the centre of the web, and a few carcasses on the concrete path below. From then on, she did exactly as her mother did. She wasn't scared of me at all, and just hung in her web when I opened and closed the gate. Like the daddy long legs, she learnt culture and the routine from her ancestor.

And then, a friend of mine who spent the seventies, eighties and nineties building an international community of Tarot readers. His life was all about building connections at a distance. In the late nineties, he died. I didn't realise. All I knew is that from a particular day onwards, every time I went outdoors, I would get covered in swarms of tiny money-spiders, hundreds of them. It would take me ages to pick them off my skin and clothing without hurting them, and place them in trees or on the ground.

Then his wife got in touch with me to tell me about his fatal accident. It happened the day the swarms of spiders started. As soon as she told me, the swarms of spiders stopped. Charlie's power animal was the spider, and he was all about connections at a distance. Spiderwebs are about connections, and money spiders are about floating distances: connections at a distance. They were probably Charlie's way of telling me that he was gone, and when I found out from his wife, the descending spiders didn't need to happen any longer.

Then there was the huntsman, a few years later and in a different but equally inconvenient house. It had rained for days. After a few days of heavy rain, a huntsman came inside, seeking relief from the interminable water. For the first day and a half he scurried around the ceiling of the living room. There were no arthropods to eat.

Then he moved to the kitchen, specifically its ceiling. Once again, he found no prey. There was plenty of human-food around, and I occasionally "accidentally" left protein-based foods in sight hoping he'd at least try them, but no. He only recognised live prey as food.

Then he moved to the bathroom after a day or two. By now he hadn't eaten anything for days, and he was getting a bit frantic. Then he spent half a day on the ceiling on the baby's room, then graduated to ours. I desperately hoped he'd come halfway down the wall so that I could gently pick him up and put him in the branch of a tree outside regardless of teeming rain, but he stuck to the ceiling. By now, he had spent more than a week indoors with no food, and, exoskeleton or not, was starting to look decidedly thin.

When the baby went to sleep, my partner decided to take advantage of the peace and grab a day-sleep as well. She threw herself on the bed, lying on her back, with one arm flung behind her, up against the wall, her hand quite high. I did whatever I needed to do in the rest of the house.

After an hour or so I checked on the baby, then checked on her. She was still in the same position, on her back, vertical arm propped up against the wall, snoring with championship skill and volume. Standing in the doorway and looking in, I noticed the huntsman.

He was still at ceiling-level, in the corner of the room nearest the bed. The thing about huntsmen, is they have huge eye-assemblages: you can see exactly what they are looking at. This one was looking at my partner's hand. He was a hungry huntsman–his focus was on food.

You could just see the thought-processes. He had spotted a creature. That creature had a leg-span about the same as his. But that creature was a lot heavier and possibly stronger than he was. It only had five legs, so it was possibly injured. He was doing small spider-calculations in his starving spider-brain: can I take it? Can I kill it before it realises I'm here and kills me instead?

I stood, and watched the simple train-of-thought in the spider's mind. I kept standing and watching, keeping myself still and quiet. My partner snored on.

The spider inched a few centimetres down the wall, then scurried back up, all the while watching the creature to gauge its reaction. Nothing. He hung at the ceiling for a while, then inched a little further down. Paused, looked, scurried back up.

He was a very, very hungry spider. This was the first thing it had seen that looked at all like food in ages. It was not a species he had seen before. Caution was called for. But he was starving. Without food, he was going to die anyway, which made the risk of being killed by the creature less of a problem. He had to take the chance.

He made his bravest move yet. He inched down, to just about fifteen centimetres from my partner's hand. It was wholly focussed on the hand. This was it. He was just working up the nerve to pounce. I stood in the doorway, watching.

Just then, my partner did a massive super-snore, one of those accompanied by a mini-convulsion and a flailing of limbs. The spider scurried up to the ceiling in terror. You could see that he had been so focussed on the hand that he had entirely missed the salient fact that the hand was attached to an arm, which was attached to a Huge Thing. Up until then, the spider hadn't noticed. He had only seen the hand itself, and its potential to be food.

See? Spiders are beautiful little characters. And think about it: without them, there would be many other insects around who would eat you, or eat your garden, or spread disease on their feet. And some, like huntsmen, hunt other spiders, specifically nasty ones like the funnel-web. Spiders are a natural part of the world, and belong here at least as much as you do, arguably a lot more. How many humans are killed by spiders in a year? Ten? Twelve? How many spiders are killed by humans each year? Fourteen million? Fifty million? Which species has the most to fear from the other one?

THE DISPOSAL UNIT'S STORY

It was just one of those days. You know the type. You wake up with a hangover, and the wife nags you in the shrillest of all possible voices. You get up, and she puts superglue in your morning coffee, prussic acid in your orange juice, then asks why you aren't eating breakfast. You miss all the green lights. You go to work, and the goddamn machine won't kick over at-bloody-all, until the boss comes over. Then it starts first time, and you get bawled out for loitering, just as the suburban trucks start rolling in. Yeah, you know the type of day.

It's a filthy hot day, the whole goddamn place stinks, and it takes at least fifty-six hours to get the day over, with smokos and lunchbreaks that feel like about thirty seconds. So you knock off; and wouldn't you think it was reasonable to go to the pub with your mates to have a couple of cold ones? Well, I would and I did.

So then, when I got home, wouldn't you know it, she goes off at me again. Like you'd think I was the devil incarnate or something. Where've you been, she shrieks, you smell like a brewery, and just how much money did you waste on booze and horses, and no you're not going to sit down and watch TV - answer me when I'm talking to you!

I tell you, after one of the worst days on record it was all a bit much. So, just to show her who's boss around here I gave her a couple of light taps on the side of the head, you know, just to calm her down and let her know I'm not to be messed with. Her whole body, all one and a half tonnes of it, folded up like a house of cards and fell heavily onto the floor. So I left her there to sleep it off, and went back to the TV just in time for the end of the news and the sport.

Afterwards I started feeling a little peckish—after all, she usually had a cooked dinner ready for me to eat as I watched the box—and I went looking for her to ask what was for dinner and when the hell was she going to give it to me. She was still in the hall where she had fallen, and she had gone a mighty funny colour. I nudged her with my foot, but she didn't even twitch. I got a bit concerned then; and, more curious than anything, checked her breathing.

No luck. Looked like she'd karked it this time. Well, silly bitch, what did she expect if she got me so riled up? Bit much to expect anyone to take that sort of crap from her. All the same, I didn't want anyone to start sniffing around. It was dark and starting to get cold outside. I went out to the shed and grabbed one of those large hessian sacks the builders had left there, and tried to fold her over and get her into it. Legs and arms kept flopping everywhere, so after a while I gave up and looked into every cupboard until I found where she had the spare sheets, took one and rolled her up in it, tying the bundle closed at both ends with twine.

Grabbing my jacket I dragged her out to the station wagon and shoved her in the back, then drove off into the night. I don't remember thinking about it–I just somehow ended up at work. Perfect, I thought, and climbed into the monster and kicked over the engine. By night it roared like the skies were falling down, a noise like I didn't expect. I held my breath, but no nosy cars came cruising by.

So I dragged the missus out by the feet–she was starting to stiffen, now, and was bloody awkward to move–and put her in the path of the dread machine. Then I put it into gear, and shoved the parcel over the edge. I jumped down and checked for her, but that far down it was hard to see. So I spent some time shoving rubbish over just like I was at work. Plenty of it, just to make sure she was good and covered. At length I killed the machine, wiped my hands on my overalls, and drove the wagon back home. Two neat scotches later I was sleeping like a baby: no bad dreams, no guilty conscience, no nothing.

At work I was more than usually hung over. Before I started, I walked casually to the edge and looked over. I had to know whether one of her fat little legs or a purple face was sticking out of the garbage. Nothing was there. I heaved a private sigh of relief, and walked away again. As far as I know nobody noticed. Sullenly I worked, stopped, smoked, worked again. At length the day ended, and a couple of us went to the pub for a drink.

I had one, then another. "Jee-sus," Tony said through the smoke and the noise. "And after last night, too! She's really going to kill you, mate!"

I smiled ruefully. It seemed the naturalest thing in the world to say: "Yeah. One more and I'll have to go or I'll be in trouble." And as I said it, it really seemed true to me. One more and I went, and when I got home I rang up for a home delivered pizza. The old cow never used to let me have them—too expensive, she said. So I had a medium special and a garlic bread, and pigged the lot in front of the TV.

No one asked any questions. One of the neighbours left a note for her under the door after several weeks, so I rang her and told her the missus was out of town, her mother was unwell and she was going to stay with her and look after her until she died, and yeah, I'd let her know how sorry the neighbour was and to come over as soon as she got back.

And that was it. That was the last time anyone asked after her at all. I'm guessing most people didn't like her any more than I did.

A week or so later I was in the pub after work, when in walked Truncheon Dave. Truncheon Dave was an interesting fellow, and someone who did interesting things for his living. An affable enough guy, but kept his cards close to his chest. And when you saw him and he was on a job he wouldn't even notice you, recognise you or anything. Total concentration. Double life, if you ask me. He had a collection of weapons, some ex-army, some ex-police, some home-made, some antique, in his toolshed. He showed them to me once, and there was pride in his eyes. I asked if they weren't expensive, and he grinned and said most of them had earned their keep. Then he said they were a tax deduction, then he clammed up. And that was all anyone had ever heard him say about his work.

I said hello, and he joined me and bought me a beer. When we finished the round I suggested buying a bottle of scotch and going into the park to sit and drink where it was quiet.

"Why?" He was immediately guarded—smart one, that Dave.

"I might have a business proposition for you, mightn't I."

"Can't hurt to talk," he said, indifferently. "You're buying." So I grabbed a bottle of Johnny Walker Red and we footed it out of there. When we got there I was going to sit under the trees, but he pulled at my sleeve. "I'd rather sit in the train station," he said. "Trees have ears, you know. I'd like to see who's listening."

I knew train tunnels had eyes, but he was probably right, they may not have ears. So instead we went into the tunnel, where we sat on the ground, backs against the tiles and each took a long swig from the bottle.

"That's better," he sighed, wiping his mouth with his sleeve. "Now, what's this business?"

I handed the bottle back to him. "Well, it occurs to me, see, that after a night's work—a hard night's work—you just might have some packages hanging around, see? Stuff you don't want anyone else to know about, right?—like in eighty or ninety kilo parcels? Well, it occurs to me too, that you might like to put a few dollars in the path of a trustworthy guy like me, who can get rid of them quickly, cleanly and quietly."

His eyes were narrow and intense, sizing me up. "Where would you get rid of them?"

"Trade secret. Wouldn't want just anyone to know. Word might get around."

"How do I know you're not going to mess me around?"

"You're the one with the hardware. Seems to me if I mess you around I'm the one in trouble, right?"

"What do you want for it?"

"Twenty."

"Couldn't afford more than three."

"Ten, then."

"Done."

"But only for easy jobs. Ones where I can get in and out again fast, no cops or witnesses. Any witnesses, I don't do the job. And soups'll be extra."

He didn't turn a hair. "Fair enough. Haven't changed your phone number? Right, I'll call you if I've got anything." We shook, and I left him with the bottle, sitting in a bleak underground train tunnel, drinking and looking just like a hobo with expensive tastes.

Sure enough, after a week or two I got a call. He named an office building. "Wallet in the pocket," he said.

"Easy access?" I asked. "The easiest." So I took the station wagon and went. A door had been forced open and left slightly ajar, and filled with nervousness I went in. There was the stiff, as obvious as possible, a wallet in its coat pocket. I took that into my possession, wrapped the parcel and dragged it into the car. Straight to work, and in half an hour it was nicely covered, as far as I could see in the dark. I went home, a little richer than I had been a couple of hours before.

Well, the first professional job was the hardest, mentally at least. Over the months he rang me seven times, and at each time there was always a parcel to get rid of that I would bulldoze into the landfill. Each of them would have a wallet or envelope in its pocket, once in its mouth, as the stiff was naked. There were never any people around, which was a bonus.

Only once did I have to remove a soup. It had been lying for weeks in a basement. I had my doubts, but I was promised fifteen grand to remove it and I didn't have to clean up the room too much, just a quick mopping. Leaving DNA behind was a part of the deal. When I went in through a window that was at ground-level from the outside and up under the ceiling inside and dropped to the floor, I couldn't believe the stench. It was discoloured, rank, crawling with maggots and blown up to huge proportions. I hadn't been expecting the swelling, and while I had expected the smell, it was worse than I'd imagined. I needed a plastic tarp and a shovel to remove it all, and the station wagon smelled off for days.

After the soup, he casually asked me over a beer if I wanted work from one of the big syndicates. I said that I'd only do it if he acted as the middle-man, if the price for a standard went up fifty percent, and if there would be no complications. I fully expected the whole thing to come apart then, but much to my surprise, apart from a steady trickle of night-work augmenting my income, I continued to keep driving the dozer at the tip and lived much as before. My bank balance grew, but not by much–I had a carry-bag in the wardrobe stuffed with envelopes and wallets.

After working at my day job one day I was talking with one of the other drivers in the pub, and he says to me did I know about the plans they had for the landfill, how they were going to level it off and sink the foundations of a five-star hotel in the garbage. He was laughing and joking about the stench of rotting garbage that would rise through these plush hotel rooms, while I was thinking privately about the stench of rotting bodies that would rise before that, and the shattered bones of reproachful eye-sockets.

I didn't say anything. So as to not make it too obvious, I kept working for a few days, then I chucked my keys on the foreman's boots and told him what he could do with my job. I went down to a travel agency last week

PTEROSAUR!

to price fares to Canada. I've always fancied snow, and the Aussie climate is too hot for me. Also, I've heard that the salmon fishing is pretty good. I could just imagine myself living in a little log cabin somewhere with a fishing rod and a sharp knife and not much else, financed by a bag full of envelopes for a few years until I get settled and accepted. All being well, I'll fly out some time next month, and early next year they will start levelling the site in preparation for putting up that bloody building.

BLUEBEARD

Once upon a time, in a land far away, a man with striking blue eyes built a castle. Heavily fortified, it had vertical bars on every window and horizontal bars on every door, and from every door handle hung a huge black padlock with its own huge black key, that hung always on a giant key-ring that he wore on his belt for the world to see. He filled the counting-house with money from floor to ceiling, he filled the treasury with jewellery and treasures beyond price from floor to ceiling, he filled the pantries with food from floor to ceiling, he filled the ice-house with meats of all kinds from floor to ceiling, he filled the granaries with wheat and rice and barley and rye from floor to ceiling. And lastly, he filled the courtyards, surrounded by high, strong stone walls, with fruit trees heavy with every kind of sweetness, and with flowering herbs of all kinds filling the air beneath the trees with the richest of perfumes.

He looked at his castle, so impregnable, and his bunch of keys, and knew that none could come in or go out without his permission. And it gave him pleasure. He looked at everything in his castle and his courtyard and knew he had everything he needed to live, and that gave him pleasure, too.

Most of all, he loved sapphires. The whole eastern corner of his treasury was filled with sapphires: pale-blue ones from Ceylon, dark-blue ones from Australia, and every shade of blue between from every country on the world. Mountains upon mountains of them gleamed in the sunlight falling across them from the high barred window. His yellow and pink sapphires were mixed with his other treasures, but after glancing at them he would always turn to his blue sapphires. And the sapphires were lit by the falling sunlight, and reflected back on his glossy, oiled beard, making it shine with a deep blue iridescence over its natural black, a blue that made his beard echo the blue of his own eyes.

The years passed and he became lonely. The gleam of treasure was not so pretty without someone else's eyes to see it. The lush sweetness of figs and dates twisted at perfect ripeness off the tree was not so sweet if he could not feed it to appreciative lips, to sweet lips.

He took to riding his dapple-grey horse through the town on market day, and talking to the stallholders and customers, but although he was open and friendly he was still the newcomer in the big castle, and the townsfolk were nervous. Month after month he came and talked, until he befriended a widow and her three grown daughters. One day he asked them if they would like to come to the castle for a feast in their honour.

The widow looked at her eldest daughter.

The eldest looked away. "I do not like him, Mother," she said.

"Why, child?"

"I do not know," she replied. "I just know that I do not think he is a nice man." And she would not go.

The widow looked at her second daughter.

The second daughter fidgeted. "Well, he's been nice to us," she said, "and his offer is generous. But I'm uneasy."

Before the widow could look at her youngest daughter, she laughed and said: "He's being more than nice to us! Look at the beautiful castle he has built, and how it reflects the sunlight off its white stone surfaces! Look at how he comes to town every market day just to talk to people, buy produce without even haggling, sometimes paying for food for the poor to take home so that they get two loaves instead of one. Look at how nice he has been to everyone, especially us, for so long! I feel we should be nice to him in return, I feel that it is unkind to repay generosity with suspicion."

So the next week the widow took her middle daughter and her youngest daughter to the feast, whilst the eldest stayed at home.

There was such merriment. The food was fresh and delicious, the bread was light and fluffy, the water was cold and cleansing. After the meal the man showed the widow and her two younger daughters around the castle, with its grand walks, its arches, its windows, its thick soft carpets, its hand-carved, comfortable furniture, the myriad colourful paintings and tapestries on the walls. And they agreed that it was a very fine home.

"Not as fine as if I had someone to share it with," he muttered under his breath.

The next week he asked them to come riding with him. The middle daughter made an excuse: seeing his fine house had not persuaded her that something was not wrong. The younger daughter came willingly, and her mother accompanied her. The women rode on two fine chestnut mares, the man on his dapple-grey gelding, its saddlebags bulging.

They rode to a clearing in the woods, with a fallen tree-trunk to sit on, and a small stream trickling through between the light and the shade. There they let the horses drink and graze, as he unpacked his saddlebags. They were filled with wonderful things to eat, including great globular oranges from his orchard, their skins the colour of embers and their juice tasting of the strength of sunlight.

And there, with the permission of the widow, he asked the youngest daughter to marry him, and when she said yes he produced from his pocket a golden ring in the shape of a lemniscate, with a diamond in one loop and the finest pale-blue sapphire in the other, and placed it on her hand.

They prepared a magnificent wedding and invited the whole village. The bride was allowed to choose any of the fabrics in his storehouse, and she chose a fabric as sparkly as the stars on a still night, overlaid on another as calmly silver as moonlight. At the wedding the second sister said maybe he wasn't as bad as she had thought; the eldest sister just looked away without saying anything. And they were married, and the youngest sister went to live in the castle, where she was very, very happy.

After some time the husband called his wife to him and told her: "I am going away on business for a while. I will be gone two weeks. Here is my keyring: you may enter every room in the castle which the black keys open, but the tiny bronze key, that is special. Do not open the lock that it fits. I could take the key with me, but I'd rather trust you. Can I trust you?"

And the young bride said he could, so he handed her the keys and said that to prevent her from becoming too lonely she could invite her family to stay for the two weeks, if she liked. So she thanked him and kissed him goodbye, and he rode away on his dapple-grey, his saddlebags bulging.

The young bride went to her mother's house, and said that the whole family could visit for two weeks. The widow had missed her, and so had her two older sisters, so they came right away, leaving a note on the table for their seven brothers, who were away at the wars, and would be coming home any day now.

They went to the castle, and the bride opened the portcullis with a great black key that turned many cogs that pulled on two chains, and led them in. For days they were happy to be together, and chattered about all the things they needed to talk about; then the eldest sister, who still didn't like the husband, asked her why she always wore the keys at her belt. So the bride told her about the promise. The two older sisters, delighted, thought it would be a great game to open every locked door in the castle and see what was behind it. They started at the attics, looking at great bundles of herbs hanging from the rafters drying, and worked their way slowly down the castle, floor by floor. It took most of the day to look at everything.

Last of all they reached the cellars, where the fine pink, yellow and purple wines were stored, and where the well that never ran dry was, for the castle to draw water. It was cool and quite dark in the cellars, the only light twinkling faintly from the top of the stairs. In the shadows there, the girls found a small door. "This must be the door that tiny bronze key opens," the middle sister exclaimed. "Shall we open it?"

"No," said the bride, definitely. She remembered how her husband had asked if he could trust her.

At the same moment the oldest sister said "Yes," and her voice was louder and she was more excited so the sisters opened the door, the youngest hanging back wishing it hadn't happened. The eldest looked in, and started crying. The middle one looked in, and fainted. The youngest didn't look in, so she never knew what her sisters had seen. She pulled them out of the doorway and slammed it shut, turning the key to lock it fast. She put the key-ring back on her belt and wiped the tears of the eldest sister, then revived the middle sister.

By the time all that was done she felt a dampness on her leg. She looked down, and found great gouts of warm, steaming blood pouring from the little bronze key down her clothes. She knew at once it was marking her untrustworthiness for her husband to see.

She and her sisters tried wrapping the key, but it still bled. They tried washing the key, but it still bled. They tried pressing it with sand, but it still bled, saturating the sand. They tried covering it with wax to seal the blood in, but still it bled. The bride was terrified, knowing that the husband only had to see the bleeding key, and he would know he couldn't trust her.

At that moment they all heard the sounds of horse's hooves on the cobblestones outside: the husband's business took several days less than he expected. The two elder sisters took their mother and fled, leaving the bride alone. Frantically she dropped the key on the floor, and kicked it under some heavy curtains. Her husband entered the room. He saw the blood on her dress, starting where the key-ring was dangling.

"Did you use the bronze key?" he asked.

She stuttered and stammered, and as she tried to start to tell him that it wasn't her fault but her sisters', he saw the pool of blood start to ooze from beneath the curtain. With a great cry, he fell on the key and picked it up, sobbing. His bride had betrayed him. She hadn't given her mother and sisters great chests of sapphires and other precious gems to take away. She hadn't emptied the gold out of the counting-houses into their waiting aprons. She hadn't even kissed the servants. She had just done the one thing she told him she could be trusted not to do.

His pain was immense. Without even knowing what he was doing he turned to her, let out a wordless roar and tried to tear the pretty lemniscate ring off her fingers.

At that moment, the seven brothers entered the room. They had gone home, seen the note, and come to the castle. Hearing their sister's screams and her husband's roars they entered the room, and seeing the blood from the key all over her dress and him pulling at her hand as soon as they came in, they waited no longer, but drew their seven shiny swords and cut him to pieces where he stood, heedless of their sister's screams for them to stop.

Many characters get vilified in fairy stories, and I think Bluebeard is one of them. The crucial thing about the many very different versions of the story is the betrayal at the end. The bride never disposed of his wealth—at the most, she showed it to his family. The murky secret in the locked room—which in earlier versions of the tale is never described let alone spelled out as the remains of previous curious wives—is the only thing the bride is forbidden. The point is not discovering that he is an evil wife-murderer—the point of the whole story is that his trust is betrayed by her and he attempts (and in most versions succeeds) in punishing her.

The role of the mother and the elder sisters, who have been edited out in some dumbed down versions, is not trivial, either. What kind of mother would let one of her daughters court a stranger, or even someone well-known—without any kind of comment or judgement passed on the suitor, negative or positive? Perhaps her passivity towards her daughter's decisions represents a feeling of being inadequately mothered. And the two older sisters represent more knowledgeable aspects of the bride herself: the middle sister, slightly uneasy about the man, can't place her finger on what's wrong. She represents a dawning sense of intuition, specifically of a looming unpleasantness in the future.

The eldest sister, older and therefore supposedly more developed, is less likely than the middle sister to be bribed or side-tracked into accepting a thing she thinks is wrong. However, at the same time, she takes the initiative in breaking the husband's prohibition on using the key, and is the first into the locked room, to see whatever lies within it. It is her choice of action, encouraged by the middle sister, that precipitates the disaster in the first place.

The story is not a fable of a gruesome murderer or the need to avoid trusting a husband. The story is about loyalty, living up to your promises, living by your word and making those around you conform to it too, if at all possible. It is about honour and integrity. The bride did not take action to open the room, but she could have taken more action to prevent her sisters opening it on her behalf. In many versions of the story we are not told what lies within the room, just that it is a terrible shock: the act of opening the door itself is more important than the contents of the room, precisely because it is a morality-tale about living by your promises.

Perhaps all the room contained was nothing. In fact, the other side of nothing—a vortex, an abyss, a deep darkness. And perhaps all who saw it, saw their own inner lives reflected in that abyss, their conscience for any wrong-doing in the past, their dread of any retribution in the future. What if every idyllic environment had a dark corner? You look into yourself at your peril.

THERE BE DRAGONS

Once upon a time in a faraway kingdom, a dragon controlled the land. He lived in a nearby volcano, coiled up on a bed of lava when he was home.

The people of the kingdom told themselves stories, because he was so large and toothy, stories about him needing to eat young girls, or he would come and burn their town down and eat everyone else.

Eventually the people forgot they were stories, and started throwing young girls into the volcano. He was appalled. He knew humans didn't have thermo-resistant skin, and watched the first couple die horribly. After that, he tried to catch them if he could, and if he managed to get them before the lava did, he'd hold them tenderly in his part-open mouth as he flew out of the kingdom to set them by a town where he knew the people weren't cruel enough to throw young girls into volcanoes.

But because the girls never came back, and because he was seen to fly after they had been thrown in, the people surmised that he was eating them and that they provided strength to him, and kept doing it. The dragon didn't like it. The girls really didn't like it–it was just one more form of systemic misogyny in an already middle-aged-white-male-centred world. But the town kept the practice up, causing grief to a lot of local families.

One day the dragon had had enough. He flew out of the volcano and circled the town a few times, looking for the best place to land. The best place turned out to be a concrete quadrangle in front of a massive building. He hoped their leader lived in that massive building, but in the event, it turned out to be only a shopping centre. However, he did get noticed as he landed in the carpark, being careful not to touch any of the cars.

People looked at him with fear.

He held his hands out to show he had no weapons, but they recoiled at the gesture, and a few ran away.

"Take me to your leader," he croaked. He hadn't had a drink before he came, and his throat was parched.

The town's mayor was summoned. He approached, quaking with fear.

"What do you want?" he asked. "We can get you more girls, if you want."

The dragon cleared his throat. "I just want you to stop throwing girls into the volcano," he said in his more melodious normal voice.

"Where do you want us to put them? Do you have a house we can bring them to?"

"What do I want with them?"

"You eat them, don't you?"

The dragon looked shocked. "Hell, no. I'm a mineralarian. The volcano gives me all my sustenance. No, I rescue the poor little things, and fly them to a town where the people aren't savages, and where they will be looked after properly, not thrown into volcanoes. As a special favour to me, can you stop doing it?"

"You don't eat them? You're sure?"

"I don't eat them, I rescue them from your cruelty. Can you stop it please?"

"Oh, okay. By the way, do you need a job?"

"What's a job?"

"It's when you do something to fill in your days."

"I snooze, mostly. Why, what did you have in mind?"

That afternoon, the mayor introduced the dragon to the town's potter. From then on the dragon still snoozed, but eight hours a day he snoozed outside the potter's workshop instead of curled up inside the volcano, where his breath fired the new pottery on racks in front of him.

The potter was happy. The town was happy. The dragon was happy. And the remaining young girls were very happy indeed. In fact, it could honestly be said that they all lived happily ever after.

GODS' NIGHT OUT

All the gods of the mountain thunderstorms
Gather together to play ten-pin bowling
On the Gods' Night Out.

Thor, old fuddy-duddy that he is,
Waits impatiently for the others outside in the cold,
And feeds the goats, stamping his feet in the clouds.

Far below, his girlfriend having taken his keys from him
And having nowhere else to escape the driving rain,
He goes to the mine where he wrestles a digger by day.

Drenched in sleet and tears, he finds ungathered ore.
He does not hear the laughter of happy storm-gods.
He is crying, that guy standing on wet copper.

Bear with me for a while. Imagine that the old gods are real, exactly as they are in the stories. Brigid blesses your hearth and heals you. Bes guards your house. Mercury looks after postal workers, parcels in transit and, oddly, marine outboard engines, at least the Mercury-branded ones. Bast scratches the ears of cats. All the gods from the older pantheons do pretty much what their publicity material says they do.

I didn't write this poem. It wrote itself, and it's up to me to figure out why it wanted to be written, and what it means.

All the gods of the mountain thunderstorms gather together to play ten-pin bowling on the Gods' Night Out.

Many workplaces have nights out. Many social groups enjoy ten-pin bowling. It's not too much of a stretch, that on a work night out, the gods might go to ten-pin bowling. Thor, loveable old god that he is, is not the only thunder god or storm god. He's in good company, with Indra, Jupiter and Jupiter's half-brother, Zeus. The Japanese Susanoo and the Mexican Cocijo are enthusiastic gods of storms and thunder, too.

Their workplaces are similar and their jobs are similar or at least overlap. They would know each other, in the way that colleagues do. They are not best friends, they are not intimate, but they know of each other, recognise each other, and acknowledge the work that the others do. And as colleagues, it makes sense that once or twice a year, they might go on a night out, a gods' night out.

To me, Thor is an old god. Heavy, bearded, possibly disillusioned. The others seem younger: more enthusiastic and less skilled, more inclined to laugh and play. They would be the drinkers, Thor would be the Designated Driver. Which makes sense, given that he has his goat-drawn cart. He is not into laughing and joking and rolling big, heavy balls down narrow lanes at skittles.

He drives them there, and has a drink with them, and exchanges some friendly words, then as they kit up and start playing, he, feeling like a square peg in a round hole, takes himself off out of the warmth and the bright lights, into the bitter snow where his goats are tethered, still in their harnesses. He makes sure they can reach some hay, and he rubs them down with rough sacking to dry them off, warm them up and make them feel loved.

Out in the quiet snow, the silence is accentuated by his being able to hear the party from a distance, the sounds of the bowling, the laughter and conversation. He is more at home out here. And he can't keep his mind off work even on a night when he is off-duty—he is a conscientious god, unlike the youngsters.

The rolling of the balls along the bowling lanes is adequate, he thinks, for making the sound of very distant thunder, for the humans below, but it is nothing like the volume of the wheels of his cart. Thor waits patiently outside in his furs with his goats, waiting for their evening out to be over and for them to stumble out and pile into his cart so he can drive them all home safely.

Then the perspective changes. *Far below, his girlfriend having taken his keys from him and having nowhere else to escape the driving rain, he goes to the mine where he wrestles a digger by day. Drenched in sleet and tears, he finds ungathered ore. He does not hear the laughter of happy storm-gods. He is crying, that guy standing on wet copper.*

We're not looking at Thor, or the world according to Thor any more. We are looking at a little human, kilometres below. Thor, the ten-pin bowling venue and all the other gods, are using the cloud-cover as their floor. The guy of these last lines, is far below those "floorboards," on the regular earth.

What do we know about him? His girlfriend has taken his keys off him. Conflict right there, and sudden homelessness, temporary or permanent. And we know it's a stormy night because Thor is out and about, which means thunder and lightning, usually accompanied by wind and rain. So the weather is going to reflect his mood. It is rainy, and he is tearful.

"He goes to the mine where he wrestles a digger by day." I live in a mining area and mines are a twenty-four hour operation, but this mine seems very different, and it insisted on being a daylight-only operation. And an operation where the machinery is bobcat-like, rather than the serious, heavy, town-sized machines we have in mines these days. Honestly, I was almost expecting a canary.

And while I'm in a coal-mining region, it seemed to be a copper mine. Copper is usually mined as its ores, chalcopyrite mostly, and malachite and azurite, all of which are beautiful in their different ways, but none of which are raw metal. Yet he is standing on fragments of raw metal, that had fallen away from the walls of the tunnel during the day's dig and had not been completely gathered up by the withdrawing bucket.

And here he is alone in the darkness, taking shelter in a mine tunnel already drenched from the process of getting in there, standing on wet copper in a thunderstorm. Normally, one is well-advised not to stand on wet copper in a thunderstorm, because wet copper is a particular friend of electricity, and lightning is wild, uninhibited electricity which has no discipline and does whatever it wants whenever it wants.

The poem has two parts: an old weather-god waiting patiently or impatiently for the younger gods to finish with their fun, and a distressed human weeping his eyes out, having no idea where to go or what to do. It wrote itself. It insisted on being written. And when I tried to edit it, to improve it, it has resisted me strenuously. I have not changed a single word since the moment it poured itself through me and out onto the paper.

THE CAT LOVER

He throws the long-suffering cat over on its back upon his lap. It is riddled again. Quietly, he searches it for the diveaway flea-sized areas of darkness on its coat, or the tiny gaps in its fur that are caused by the presence of a root-level flea.

Once the flea is found, the technique of killing it is very important. He once used to have a glass of water at hand in which to drown them. They would flounder around on top of the water until they got to the sides of the glass, then they'd crawl up and jump away. No good. So he started forcibly submerging them.

Some would bob up to the surface, but most would sink to the bottom. There they would kick helplessly at nothing until they stopped moving. Naturally enough, he thought they were dead when they stopped moving, but this was not the case. It appeared that they could live for several hours like that, in a form of hibernation, until something happened to rescue them. That something was usually him throwing the glass of water down the sink, when they would stay on the sink's surface, recover rapidly, then bound away brimming or seething (which do fleas do, he wondered, brim or seethe?) with vengeful fury, determined to bite fifteen times as hard.

No, drowning would definitely not do. Who needs angry fleas? He'd rather have them placid.

So then he did some reading and manufactured herbal flea collars, using weird and wonderful herbal oils that were supposed to be insect-repellents, and saturating a strip of cloth in the evil-smelling brew, then tying it around the hapless (and vigorously protesting) cat's neck. From the initial moment of contact with fur, he imagined he could hear the fleas laughing hysterically at this joke.

No, being ideologically sound and using herbal flea collars was just not sufficient, even if it was morally pleasing. He went out and bought real a flea collar.

For a few days the cat was relatively untroubled. It scratched occasionally. Obviously the strongest of the fleas were surviving whatever foul toxins would eventually poison his beloved. Then the fleas started mutating. More and more became resistant to the poison, and more and more bit the cat savagely. He drew the line when they started biting him as well.

And even biting the cat was a bit much. After all, he paid good money for catfood. Damn good money, considering he was on the dole. The fortnightly payment would only buy so much, after all. A goodly proportion of that catfood was used up by the cat's body to replace the blood necessary to its wellbeing that the fleas had drunk. So he was really spending money to feed fleas, when he thought about it. He didn't like that idea.

He went to a pet shop to buy some gamma wash. Some gamma radiation might just kill the bastards, he reflected, teetering on the edge of nuclear warfare. "Gamma wash? No, have this Diawash," said the pet shop owner. "The chemicals are just the same and it's much cheaper. Gamma wash are pricing themselves out of the market." So he bought the Diawash.

Evil-smelling stuff. Clear in the bottle, it turned corpse-white when mixed with the appropriate quantity of water. He had to admit it was economical. He grabbed the cat and rubbed a Diawash-saturated rag all over it energetically. It wailed despairingly and flailed with wickedly-equipped limbs. He bled, Diawash getting into his wounds and itching madly. The fleas perished. He showered.

The following week the cat was riddled again, so he bathed it again. Again it fought–this time it knew what was coming. As it sadly licked itself dry in front of the radiator, an expression of distaste on its Egyptian-Temple-Cat features, he noticed several drunken or convulsing fleas that were still alive and two that didn't seem to be affected at all, jumping from its wet fur. The cat started snuffling and wheezing, and spending a lot of time at the litter tray.

The third week the initial fight was even more enormous, and the fleas merely thumbed their noses at the poisonous bath. It was more toxic to the cat. The fourth week, there was an enormous population explosion immediately following the bath. The fleas had evolved.

Perhaps it had become an integral part of their environment, or worse still their lifestyle. Maybe they had mutated enough to need it as they needed blood for egg manufacture. If it had become a part of their breeding cycle, shouldn't he discontinue using it?

Yet they still bred. He discontinued using it. There wasn't much left in the repertoire for killing fleas any more. He was reduced to the oldest, most traditional method of all. This consisted of throwing the hapless puss over his lap, picking out the visible fleas, and crushing them between his fingers. This was slow, even with a fine-toothed comb to drag for them. Also, more fleas were trawled than he could kill before they escaped back into the fur.

He found that crushing them with his fingers left them unscathed unless his fingers were moist enough to create friction and he rolled them to break their legs. He had somehow to position them on one thumbnail and crush them with the other thumbnail. This was slow work.

He throws the long-suffering cat over on its back upon his lap. It is riddled again. Quietly, he searches it for the diveaway flea-sized areas of darkness on its coat, or the tiny gaps in its fur that are caused by the presence of root-level fleas.

A DISGRACE OF ANGELS

Normally the collective noun for angels is choir, a choir of angels. But these ones had put aside their harps and were looking rather less than choral as they hung their heads in shame. What would a more applicable collective noun be—an embarrassment of angels? A disgrace of angels? I glared at them. They avoided my eyes and tried to shuffle behind each other.

"Honestly," I went on, "what were you thinking?"

More shuffling, and a sublingual murmuring of "Yes, miss" and "sorry, miss."

"I mean, I'm a human. I come complete with Original Sin, and even I know it was wrong."

When a human blushes, they feel hot, and they go pink. When an angel blushes the heat radiates everywhere, and they shine so brightly that either closed eyes or sunnies are called for. And that's just one. Imagine what it's like when there's a whole bunch of them blushing in front of you. I continued relentlessly.

"Michael! Step forward!"

An ashamed little angel, shoulders stooped and wings dragging, didn't so much come forward, as found himself forward when the rest fell back behind him.

"Have you got anything to say for yourself?"

"No, miss. Sorry, miss."

"I mean, look at you! Your robe is dirty, you still have bloody sump oil on your right wing! What the what!"

"It was all about the children, miss," whispered Michael, the very epitome of angelic misery. For a brief instant his head flickered into the crocodile head of Sobek, then he regained control of himself and looked like a Renaissance angel again. "I had to protect the children."

"Yes, I understand that is your traditional role." My voice was iron. "What I would like to know is, what made you think any child would benefit from your draining the oil out of that man's car?"

Michael looked even more miserable. His halo had faded almost out of existence by now. "He might have been a child abductor, miss. I couldn't take the chance."

"And he might have been pursuing a child abductor who had a child chained up in the boot of his own car. You just don't know, do you. Do you?"

"No, miss."

"So you drained his sump, so that when he next started the engine, it would seize up. Is that an angelic thing to do?"

"No, miss."

"Get outta here. I don't want to see you again until you have cleaned yourself up, body and soul."

I looked at the remaining huddle of quaking angels. "And you lot! You encouraged him, didn't you! You cheered him on! I mean, just because he's the only one who's bothered to learn anything about technology from after the sixteenth century doesn't make him a hero!"

"No, miss. Sorry, miss."

"Did not one single one of you have a moment's thought that this behaviour might be less than ideal? Then slightest flicker of a thought?"

They all, as one, looked down at their feet. Their traditionally golden sandals had turned into rough, brown leather sandals, to match their behaviour. "Sorry, miss. We'll try better next time."

"And you. Phosphorus." He obediently stepped forward. "I don't suppose you can explain exactly why you burnt down that building? Arson? Really? Are angels arsonists, now?"

He tried. He tried gamely. "I'm Phosphorus. I'm meant to burn." For a moment his angel form disappeared and he presented as a sheet of flame, a couple of metres high and a centimetre thick. I blinked, and he was an angel again. An embarrassed angel.

I did my best withering voice. "No, you're Phosphorus. A mineral named after you is meant to burn, not you. You are meant to be an angel, and do angelic things. What happened?"

"So many people thought about it burning down …"

"So you thought you'd help them? Think about it. They're disaffected teenagers who'd rather be hanging out at the shops or surfing or gaming than sitting in a classroom. Of course they want their school to burn down. That doesn't mean you should do it. Think like an angel, not a hormone-affected teenager!"

"Yes, miss. Sorry, miss."

"Give me your tinderbox. Now get over there and help with the clean-up effort. And try to look like a random human volunteer!"

"Yes, miss." A nondescript forty-something man wearing jeans, trainers and a faded yellow tee-shirt walked away.

"Uriel? I don't suppose as the angel of knowledge, you have any complicity in this? For forks' sakes, schools are all about knowledge! It's your job to protect them."

"Yes, Miss."

"And while I'm at it, Gabriel. You've been fast-tracked on the angelic leadership path. You are close with the Boss. Is your idea of leadership to stand around and do nothing while a couple of your staff trash a car and a school? What the hell, mate. I understand you gave them all a night off, last night. Did you not think to remind them that they are angels and role models? Instead of being role models, they went off and behaved like a bunch of ... a bunch of ... a bunch of bloody NRL players! I hold you responsible. What have you got to say?"

"Sorry, miss."

"Sorry? I'm sick of hearing it. Sorry doesn't hack it. How would you like it if I went over your head and spoke to the Boss?"

Gabriel turned pale. "Oh, please don't do that!"

I lowered my voice dangerously. "I will if it happens again. And may I assure you, I'm not bluffing. Just remember what happened to Lucifer. And you'd better hope I never die, because he has a restraining order on me so I can't go to hell. If I die and go to heaven, I'll be watching you every moment of every day for all eternity. Do you want that?"

"No, Miss."

So pull your finger out of your arse, and start behaving like a leader, not a ringleader! And the rest of you, "–they flinched visibly–" stop behaving like out-of-control brats and start behaving like angels. I've had about enough of the lot of you."

I threw one last glare at them, then turned around and stalked off, radiating disapproval and dignified outrage.

THE HAIRCUT

Cold early morning fog always pleased Sooz, and this one was a really thick one. She sat on her back deck armed against the cold with her dressing gown and a cup of steaming tea, watching the whiteness swirling amongst her garden beds like attenuated eels in a mating frenzy. The fog blessed her cheeks with infinitely gentle, cold-lipped kisses. The tea cooled as she slowly sipped it, until the cup felt warm to her cold fingers and cool to her warm lips.

When she had had enough she went inside, and poured the remainder of it down her sink. She felt too fluffy. She hated being fluffy. She needed a haircut, to become unfluffy again. One of the things she really liked about having extremely short hair, was that under the shower you could feel every single drop individually hitting your head, and it felt just as if the water was effervescing on your head. She hadn't felt that sensation for a long time. Her hair was freshly shampooed. Perhaps it was time.

Remembering the last one, and how it concertinaed into a long line of them that were equally unpleasant, she procrastinated. Still, if she didn't do it today, she probably wouldn't tomorrow. And she was just so unpleasantly fluffy. So, in the late morning, she drove to the town's one shopping mall. There had been two swish-looking salons there, luxuriously appointed so they could charge top dollar, plus a much plainer cheap-and-cheerful place simply referring to itself as a hairdresser's, not a salon or a studio. It had been there that she'd had every haircut since moving to the town.

And there she returned—or tried to. But it had gone! Much against her better judgement, she went to the studio. They looked down their noses at the idea that they might squeeze her in, checked their book, and offered a time four days in the future. The salon offered a time five days in the future. Sooz didn't operate that way. As someone to whom time was an unreal chimera flickering uncertainly in front of her, she couldn't commit to things like that.

She went home, picked a few leaves from her garden vengefully, wrapped them up in a flatbread with some cheese, and chewed it as viciously as she would have liked to chew up those young fashion-victims with her words.

Now that she had become aware of her hair as a problem, though, it wouldn't go away. She could feel it on her ears. She could feel it on her neck. Her fingers kept rising to run themselves through it involuntarily. It was almost long enough to get caught in the hinges of her glasses and break off into two little tufts, as it used to do many years ago when she kept it longer.

Why the hell couldn't you just stop your hair growing when you achieved the perfect haircut?

She tried to work, but nothing turned out. Her hair was annoying her. Eventually she closed the laptop, grabbed her keys, and climbed into the car. The engine purred quietly as she drove into the town centre. There must be a hairdresser somewhere. She parked, and started walking along the outdoor shopping strip.

There was. Her heart sank when she looked at it. It wasn't an unpretentious hairdresser—it was an upmarket hair and beauty studio, all silver furniture and silver fake trees and black tiles with silver flecks. There were two women there, one of them very young. The apprentice. There were no customers. Sooz felt as if it was the right kind of place to keep well away from, but her hair was really annoying her now, more with every minute. Against her better judgement, she walked in.

The young girl smiled a professional smile at her. "How can I help?"

"Just a quick buzz-cut."

The girl made a show of taking time to check the computer, frowning slightly. "We can probably squeeze you in right now."

Sooz refrained from glancing pointedly around the empty room. "Thanks."

"Before we start, can I just get you to fill in our introduction form? Just so we get to know you."

Sooz didn't see why they needed to get to know her to cut her hair. Okay, a doctor might need to get to know her to have some idea how to treat her. An architect might need to get to know her to be able to design a house to her taste. But a hairdresser? If she went to buy takeaway food, she thought, they wouldn't insist on her filling in an introductory form before selling her hot chips or tabbouleh. She says what she wants, they give it to her, she gives them money. She should just be able to tell a hairdresser what she wants, then pay them when they give it to her.

But no. It was a full A-4 sheet of questions. Run away now? No, she really, really needed that haircut. The first question was her name. She wrote "Margaret Davis." Title. It gave her the choice between Miss, Mrs and Ms. How sexist—a woman couldn't hold the title Professor, or Doctor? Captain, Colonel or General? Air Marshall or Admiral? Contrary to instructions, she didn't choose one. And thus, down the form, she wove a web of half-truths and omissions. By the end of it, not only was her hair uncomfortable, but she was seething with silent fury at the embedded sexism and total lack of regard for personal privacy that the whole of the form demonstrated.

She handed the form back to the girl. The older woman had disappeared, she noticed.

"Would you like a coffee or tea?"

That will immediately inflate the price, thought Sooz. Aloud, she said "Yes, please."

The tea arrived in a silver cup with black flecks, to reverse-match the benchtops and floor tiles. It was as tepid as if it had been made with water from the hot tap. As soon as she put it down the older woman arrived, and led her to a chair in front of a mirror.

"What would you like today?" she asked, in carefully modulated tones.

"As I said before, a buzz-cut. A number three comb all over. Just get rid of the lot of it."

"Are you sure? A lot of people ask for that, then don't like how it makes them look."

"For starters, that is how I've had my hair cut for over twenty years. And I don't spend my whole day looking at myself, so I really don't care how I look. Please. Can you just do it?" Sooz could hear a slightly whiney, beggy tone in her voice at the end that she didn't like. She hoped the woman didn't notice.

The hairdresser tilted her head forward, and started working upwards from her neck. "What else are you doing today?" Sooz dodged the question.

"What have you got planned for the weekend?" She dodged that one, too.

"Are you married or divorced?"

"What do you do for work? Or are you retired–what did you do for work?"

"Do you have children? Grandchildren?"

"Have you lived in town all your life, or when did you move here?"

"Have you had Covid yet?"

And on, and on, and on, with intrusive, personal questions. Sooz hated every one of the questions. She was there for a haircut. In order to have her hair cut at all, she needed to allow a stranger to stand too close to her and keep touching her head. Wasn't that invasive enough, without her privacy being violated as well? The last hairdresser Sooz had seen in a few times, had started off the same way, but Sooz had managed to train her into just cutting her hair in silence. This woman didn't seem to shut up with the interrogation despite Sooz's obvious unwillingness to participate.

Sooz squeezed her eyes shut and suffered, forming monosyllabic replies or none at all. The hair fell around her, light and silent, mouse-brown when it should have been grey. Eventually the woman put down the clippers, picked up a brush, and brushed her neck.

"If you just walk over to the first basin and sit down, Crystal will wash your hair. Then when it's wet I'll cut away any stray hairs for you."

That was going to add to the bill, too. "I don't want it washed. It's just been washed. If you need it wet, can't you just use a spray bottle?" The words "like everyone else" remained unsaid.

"Gosh no! That will never do! You won't regret it."

Sooz felt a strong urge just to drop some money on the floor and run away, screaming, into the sunlight of insanity. But society in general, and her mother in particular, had trained her to be socially acceptable, or at least to fake the appearance of it. Feeling doomed, she stood and headed to one of the chairs with a basin.

A jet of cold water hit her head. She jumped. The water became a little too hot. A huge amount of shampoo, perhaps enough for someone with ankle-length hair, was smeared all over. Then the rubbing started. How much rubbing did short, thin hair need? It went on.

And on.

And on, and on, and on.

Sooz sat there alternately gripping the arms of the chair or balling her fists, her face twisted in a series of grimaces, her whole body tense. Surely the girl would notice! But no. After a long and dreadful time, the water was turned on again. She almost relaxed–they had finished with her. But the rinse wasn't about getting shampoo out of the hair, apparently. Again, it went on for ages. And there was far too much unnecessary and unpleasant hand-to-head contact of the rubbing kind.

Then a break. Was this the end? Nope. Another great quantity of slimy stuff, which she hoped was conditioner. Had nobody taught these people that super-short hair didn't need conditioning as it never developed dry ends?

She sat there exactly as she had during the shampooing and rinsing, tensed and grimacing, waiting for the ordeal to end.

Another prolonged rinse. Only another ten or fifteen minutes of unnecessary head-rubbing: Sooz judged that she could just about survive that, without having to scream. She gritted her teeth and endured.

As soon as the hands retreated and the water stopped, she went to stand up. Three wet fingertips touched her on one shoulder, pushing her back. She was aghast. More? Yes, more. More slime on her head. The girl had done a double-shampoo of her scrupulously clean hair, and was now conditioning it. Sooz felt like a dog tied to a leash in a backyard or locked in a crate indoors without toys, shelter or even water, its owners gone to work, wondering if this hell was ever going to end.

Probably twenty minutes later, it did. Sooz was finally released, and could stand up. The apprentice disappeared out the back. The hairdresser was at the till. Sooz supposed she had better pay them for the ordeal they had put her through. After all, her hair was satisfactorily short, and they had used a lot of very expensive products in the wash.

"How was that?"

Sooz's jaw was still tense–it took her a moment to get sounds out. "Horrible."

The hairdresser's face was a combination of disbelief and disappointment. "How so? What was wrong?"

"I'm not a fan of being unnecessarily touched by strangers." She didn't go on to say that she knew having her head touched during the cut was necessary, but everything after that had been pure, spiteful torture. She paid, smiled politely, and left. She was nothing if not polite.

As she walked down the street to her car, she decided that next time she felt unacceptably fluffy, she'd go back to the same place. She'd walk in, and before they'd even said hello, she'd lay down her terms. She pictured herself saying:

"I intend to pay you extra if you cut my hair on my terms. These are my terms. Firstly: do not talk to me! My life is none of your business. If I want to chat to a friend, I'll ring a friend. If I need psychotherapy, I'll make an appointment with a psychotherapist. From you, what I want is a haircut, and nothing else. Secondly, do not insist that I have my hair washed! It goes without saying that if I go to have a haircut, my hair will already be freshly shampooed. I realise you need to touch my head during the actual cut, but when someone presents with clean hair, washing it is just unnecessary physical contact, and having strangers touch me without my consent is invasive, unpleasant and downright upsetting. If you can agree to these terms, we can do business. If you can't, I'll book a motel, and drive five hours each way to the town where I used to live, to have my hair cut."

Sooz wondered how the hairdresser would take that. Not well, she imagined. She probably prided herself on personal service (talking) and head massages (the unnecessary ordeal at the basin). Imagining the expression on the hairdresser's face at some time in the future amused her. And she had to admit her head did feel delightfully light and unfluffy. By the time she reached her car, there was a spring in her step and she was whistling cheerfully.

LOVE LETTER TO LONDON

Dear London,

It has been thirty-four years since I landed at Heathrow and found my way into your heart without money, friends or bookings. Today? Unthinkable.

I remember the beers I pulled, the boys who gave me a roof over my head, the quirky little bookshops and second hand dealers, each with its own smell. I remember my first taste of eel. I miss eel.

There were even some cobblestoned streets remaining, back then. Do you still have cobblestones? I would love to think you do.

I spent a Christmas there in you–remember? A cold Christmas, but not the snowy Christmas you put into all your movies. Still, it was cold enough to bite right into my bones. I was sleeping with a young boy who lived in an attic in somebody else's house. He had a mattress on the floor and a fireplace. We ate out a lot that week: fish and chips, pie and peas, and so much of the eel I kept insisting on, knowing I would never find it back home.

Christmas Eve: we counted our remaining cash together. We had enough for a bottle of tequila, to celebrate. We had enough for a bag of coal, to keep warm. We did not have enough for both. He looked at me. I looked at him.

Christmas Day: we stayed in bed, wearing every item of clothing we owned, and had tequila with toast for breakfast and lunch. It was a grand romance–it lasted nearly a fortnight. But you, London, I was never untrue to you. You came first in my heart, before the boys, before the tequila.

You were in my heart when I had saved enough to go to Wales to look at Chun Quoit. You were in my heart when I went to Cornwall to look at Tintagel. You were in my heart when I nearly went to Scotland to look at Billy Connolly, with my youthful certainty that coincidence works my way, and if I were to set foot on Glasgow he and I would find ourselves at the same place at the same time. It was still winter. I'm so glad I didn't go to Scotland.

But you were most in my heart when it was time to go, when I made my way to Heathrow, and to the correct departure gate. I didn't look back–there was nobody seeing me off. I sat and waited as the plane sat and waited. I listened to the safety demonstration. I leaned my forehead against the window as we taxied to the end of the runway.

At last the Flying Kangaroo took off, leapt into the sky with a stomach-yawing turn, and sped away from you. I looked at your rooftops, then your stain on the landscape, then the clouds covering you.

Oh, London! How I loved you! How I've missed you! Tell me I can come back and rest in your arms, now I am old.

Yours,
The Traveller

THE SILK ROAD

The Silk Road has provided a good income for many traders over time, and I am one of them. It was late at night: I went into the Golden Arches, used the bathroom, bought a coffee, sat in a corner and waited.

Most nights, this will yield nothing. Sometimes, I will get lucky. This was one of those times. I'd been there, nursing my coffee and avoiding the cold of the night, for about twenty minutes when she came in. Jeans, worn gold sandals, tee-shirt, a grubby pink backpack slung over one shoulder. She was shivering convulsively in her utterly inappropriate clothing, completely unsuited to a cold Autumn night. She had to walk right past me to get to the Ladies. I kept looking down.

When she emerged I caught her eye and slung her my warmest smile, the one that earns me the dollars. She hesitated and smiled back shyly. She couldn't have been more than twelve or thirteen.

"You look cold." I kept my voice soft and sympathetic. "Do you have enough money for a hot drink and some food?"

"Not really." She sounded nervous. But if she was afraid of strangers, she should have stayed home.

"I have money. What do you want?"

"Cheeseburger, fries. Double strength hot chocolate. Ta."

"That'll warm yer. Stay here and mind the table for me."

I returned with two burgers, two cups and a family-sized fries.

"Thanks. I can't pay you."

"You don't have to. That amount of money is nothing to me now. I'm guessing you don't have a lot."

We ate in silence for a while.

"Why's a pretty girl like you out all alone on such a cold night?"

"My stepfather."

"He hits you?"

"No, not hitting. My mum loves him, but he does bad stuff to me."

Better and better—she's already had some basic training, then. Aloud, I said: "That sounds awful. You probably need time away from home. Have you got somewhere to stay?"

She sank in her chair, looking miserable. "No."

"You know, I might have a friend who could help with somewhere to stay for a while." An employee wiping the next table glanced at us. All she would have seen was a father taking his daughter out for a late-night burger. When she moved away I went on: "It's not going to be glamorous, mind. But it's out of the cold. In the past I've sent other girls there, when they were homeless or missed the last train home or something."

It worked. She looked a little more comfortable with me. She thought I had helped others. I didn't lie to her, I just didn't describe what their lives became afterwards. It's the same old story every time.

"Thanks, mister. What's your name?"

"Steve," I lied. I was working my way through the alphabet. "What's yours?"

"Angie." Anything less angelic would be hard to imagine, with her greasy hair hanging beside her face. "Nice to meet you, Angie. Now, you eat a few more of those chips while I go outside and phone them, okay?"

I made the call. They'd have the cash counted out and bundled up for me when I arrived. She trusted me now, because I hadn't looked at her underdeveloped tits or tried to touch her. I went back in, finished my drink, and helped her eat the last of the chips.

As we walked to the car she looked up at me and beamed. "Thanks, Steve. I'll never forget this."

No, I bet you won't, kid, I bet you won't. Aloud, I said: "It's a pleasure."

The building didn't look anything special: one of a row of inner-city terraces with a small brass name-plate she wouldn't have noticed that said "IN THE PINK." The first stop on the Silk Road. A girl who had obviously worked there for some time, with all the spirit whipped out of her, let us in. She smiled at Angie. Her eyes were empty, as Angie's would be one day.

"You need a shower, doll. Come with me." She led Angie away.

A moment later she was back. She opened the safe and handed me a fat envelope. I stuck it in my jeans pocket without checking it. "Ta. I want first go at her. Right after her shower." The girl shrugged.

Fifteen minutes later, she led me to one of the locked rooms and let me in. There was Angie, clean hair and shiny skin, in a room that was wall-to-wall bed, wearing a black negligee and looking scared again. There was no sign of any of her personal possessions.

"Steve, I don't like it here. I—"

"Shut up, bitch," I said, pushing her back on the bed. "Open your fucking legs." It was time for some serious training. I for one don't mind teaching a dirty little whore her place in life. Breaking them in at least gives them a career path. They won't see any money, but they'll have a roof over their head and regular meals, which is exactly what she wanted when we met. And I can honestly say there is nothing more delicious than subduing and then punishing a girl who is trying to fight back as hard as she can.

As I locked the door behind me on a snivelling wreck of a girl, it tickled me to think her stepfather might come here and use her. And if he did, he would never tell anyone or try to get her out. He'd get a thrill from the secret, for sure, while appealing with her mother on TV for her to come home.

When she started looking less fresh, they'd sell her on. To street pimps, to Asian slave-traders, to Saudi brothels servicing international diplomats, or to the captains of cargo ships to pleasure the crew and be dumped in a foreign country without language skills or papers, where if she was really out of luck, she'd end up in a Third World prison, to pleasure guards who worked long shifts, and when she was unappealing even to them, to be thrown in with violent prisoners who hadn't seen a woman in years.

She can count herself lucky. She's at the beginning of an adventure. The Silk Road can take her anywhere.

THIS IS NOT A GHOST STORY

The living are annoying. It is so hard to get them to pay attention to anything. From the termites in their timber-framed house to the leak in the sewage pipe as it leaves the house—which is why the tree out the back always looks so healthy—to the fact that they keep walking through me!

I hate that most of all. Have they any idea how badly it tickles? Why can't they be at least a little courteous, and walk around me, or give me time to get out of their way? But I can hardly whine. These days, I have a better li- … er, existence, than they do.

At the Point of Decision, I thought briefly, and decided to hang around. Now I'm not entirely sure why. I originally thought it had something to do with love and attachment. But, surprisingly, it turns out that even the most altruistic love is a body-thing, not a self-thing. As the memory of being weighed down by flesh becomes more distant, my once-intense love of these people also changed gradually from a reality to a memory. I can say to myself that I love them, but that is only sentiment, and loyalty to past emotions.

But I'm still enjoying experiencing the physical world from a non-physical perspective. It is so nice to be entirely surrounded by gravity, to sense it and know it's there, and not to be pulled down by it all the time, dragging on your body so much that it exhausts your soul. It's good to drift through walls instead of walking through doorways, and informative, too, to see the wiring, insulation, plumbing and yes, termite damage, as you go. Humans never experience a house like this. They just pray that it will keep the weather out.

The Point of Decision, itself, was interesting. Gabriel presented as an enormous arthropod, two-thirds the size of the planet, with an unconscionable number of legs and antennae, and even more eyes. His joints clicked loudly as he moved, and his carapace shone a rich chestnut colour.

What, you thought angels were human-shaped? Let me tell you, there are hundreds of millions of arthropods on earth for every single human and most of them are significantly happier. Who do you think God really favours?

We had all the time in the world. I admired the engineering of his joints. I considered my decision. And I stayed here. I stayed here to watch my offspring visit, panic, and call an ambulance. I didn't see the point. I'd been dead for a while at that stage, panicking achieves nothing. I was room-temperature and stiff, my tongue was protruding, and the saliva that had dribbled from my mouth had hardened into crispy flakes on my cheek.

I kept watching them. I was happy that I had not given anyone the password to my phone—some of my secrets would die with me. I was happy they remembered my wishes and elected not to have religionists doing their stuff when they disposed of my body. I was deeply unhappy that they had a memorial in some dreary function room somewhere, with too much alcohol and too much food that included not enough sushi, and everyone got up and told lies about my life and my talents, and even more blatant lies about how they'd loved me.

People who had barely tolerated me until I stopped breathing. People who hadn't even pretended to tolerate me until I stopped breathing. People who drank toasts to me in champagne. I always hated champagne. How disrespectful can you be?

And then the kids went to the house and ransacked it. One of them took all my pretty lights and jewellery. Another went through my kitchenware and my collection of sculptures, discarding some of my favourites and keeping unexpected ones. And so it went on. Most of my furniture, which was in good condition, went into a skip outside. What—they couldn't hold a simple garden sale, let someone else give them money and enjoy the furniture? They had to pay money to have it carted away and dumped in landfill? I frothed at them and shouted at them, but none of them heard. All the psychic sensitivity of half a house-brick, each one of them.

Strangely, my one regret was that I'd washed up that day in the mid-afternoon, then eaten and drunk in the evening. I considered there wasn't enough washing-up to be worth a sinkful of water, so I left it for the next day. There never would be a next day, not in my body. I just confirmed my family's belief that I lived like a pig. While you're living, you expect to have plenty of regrets when you die, about things left undone and words left unsaid. But no, all I regretted was the dirty dishes.

After the house was emptied, I stayed in it for a while. I had spent decades loving that house, so it seemed like the place to stay. But it was boring. Then strangers moved in, with strange furniture and belongings. Yeah, no. Not my people at all.

So I started hanging around the people I had loved in life. They were getting on with things: working, raising children, playing music, and going on weekends away, mostly on my money. I mean, I didn't begrudge them that, but it would have been nice to have at least a cursory acknowledgement, a thank-you-Mum-for-leaving-us-money. Instead, they acted as if I didn't exist. As if I'd never existed.

This is not a ghost story. It's not as if I'm a ghost, exactly. I don't wear a sheet or rattle chains. I'm just at a loose end, with my feelings fading away and my memories of life becoming less important. I think I might schedule another appointment with that arthropod and see what else he can organize. Otherwise, eternity is going to be pretty boring.

WATCHING TV

The people of the Shetland Islands are a fierce race with flashing eyes, who think nothing of driving their cars onto boats to get anywhere, and wearing so many layers that they can barely move. I turned away from the large-screen TV with its outsized Douglas Henshall playing the old Broken Cop trope, to face the small unbroken Scot in front of me, quivering with Pictish rage.

"I found a spade under your bed this morning. We have to talk."

I'm not one to back down in the face of Pictish rage, or even Viking rage. She had plenty of both. "Yeah? What were you doing in my room?"

"Findin' the bloody spade!"

I said nothing. She let the silence lengthen, then went on: "A normal person, even a normal *Australian* person, and they're weird, keeps spades in the outdoor shed. What's it doin' under your bed?"

I smiled in what I hoped was a disarming way. "When you bury a body, you need to hide the evidence."

"You know, I'm no' entirely sure that's a joke."

"Oh come on! If I buried a body, do you think I'd incriminate myself by storing the spade under my bed?"

"I don't know. You're stupid enough."

I tried to look past her outrage to the screen. "Can we talk about this at the end of the episode? I really don't want to miss it."

"We're talkin' about somethin' serious, and you want to watch Teeveeeee?" Her voice went up an angry octave.

"Sorry." I tried to look contrite. "I suppose you want me to come clean?"

"That's exactly what I do want."

I sighed. "Okay. Well, I pulled up a few of the floorboards in my bedroom, and found a gap between the two foundation slabs. So I'm digging a cellar. In between times, I'm cleaning up the dirt and resting the floorboards back in place. Wanna see?"

"Sure."

We both went into my room. I pulled up a couple of floorboards and she bent over to look into the darkness. As quickly as I could I grabbed the spade with both hands, braced myself, and swung.

PTEROSAUR!

I knew it would be an extraordinary day when I went outside for the first cigarette, and idly watched a perfectly formed brown pterosaur the length of my thumb dart by, doing the aeronautic dance of any small flying thing hunting for smaller flying things.

Most people would be astonished to see such a thing. I was only amused. But then, most people knew pterosaurs only from David Attenborough's sensationalizing of the more charismatic giant species, while I was happier to have the modern era invaded only by one of the tiny species.

Just as that thought flickered through my mind the pterosaur did a hard stop in mid-air and glared at me, hovering close enough to my face to create a hint of a breeze on my cheek. I felt sensations of hunger. "Is that you?" The slight movement of air created by my speech touched the little dinosaur, and she rocked slightly, arching her back and beating her wings to compensate and stay in place.

In reply she glared more pointedly at me.

"Hey, it's my era, not yours," I answered. "And my home, not yours. You're the stranger here. Don't our modern insects taste right to you?"

She projected a downcast feeling at me. She was always going to make herself understandable to me, I could see that already.

I made a decision. "You're a protein-eater, aren't you? Come inside, I'll see what I've got in the fridge. Just don't shit anywhere!"

I felt the anticipation. She did a nice double barrel-roll, then zoomed upwards and out of sight. I felt little claws grasp my tangled hair, and what can only be described as tiny fingernails gently scratching my scalp. There was no weight to her. I put out the cigarette and walked as evenly as I could into the house and to the kitchen.

"Now then ... what have I got in here. A packet of thawing chunks of red meat. You can't have those, they're for the casserole. Cheese. Cheese?"

I took the foil-wrapped block out of the fridge, unwrapped it, and shaved a fragment off a corner. The pterosaur took flight, did a lap or two of the kitchen just from exuberance, and landed on the edge of the cutting board. She walked on her elbows in the ungainly way of pterosaurs to the piece I'd cut off, and sniffed it carefully. Walked around it, prodded it with an elbow, sniffed again. She looked at me with dejection.

"Not happy with cheese?" I re-wrapped the block and ate the fragment. "What else can I find in here?"

Half a chicken sandwich, that I'd lost interest in. It had tomato and snow-peas as well, and the bread had been spread with mashed avocado. Sitting in the fridge overnight, one of the pieces of bread had gone soggy with tomato juice. I pulled it out, still on last night's sandwich plate.

I peeled off the foil covering the plate and pulled a bit of chicken out of the corner. It was partly green with mashed avocado. I doubted she had ever tasted cooked chicken before, but hey, it was protein. She sniffed it with visible trepidation. I felt her wariness, then felt her hunger overcome it. She braced herself, and took a generous bite out of it. An instant later she spat it out and took to the air, circling my head and making little high-pitched screams.

Not chicken then, or possibly not the nasty plant-based taste of the avocado. What else did I have?

Eggs. I had eggs. I took one out, cracked it without fully opening it, and placed it on a plate.

She gave me an instant look of horror, without even bothering to sniff first. What kind of a species was I, that I would eat eggs? How would I feel if someone offered me a refrigerated foetus as food?

"Point taken, little creature," I said aloud, and cracked the egg properly into a glass which I covered and put back in the fridge for future use. "I think we've exhausted my current protein supplies."

Another pterosaur-scream, different to the chicken-and-avocado one, and suddenly she was diving to the floor. A cockroach. A cockroach had foolishly crawled in through a crack in the skirting board. She leapt on it feet-first like an eagle, then brought down her strong jaws and bit right through its carapace. Once it stopped struggling, she settled down to feed.

She liked cockroaches! Fantastic! I could see a future for our relationship–I loved the idea of a house-pet who would rid an old house of cockies. I boiled the kettle, and went to get dressed for work. When I returned, the cockroach was only a scattering of wings and chewed legs, and the little pterosaur was sunning herself on the windowsill, presumably to find the energy to digest. Her tummy was swollen with food.

We smiled at each other as I gulped down my tea. "Come on," I said. "Time for work." On cue, she flew to my left shoulder and perched there, as if we'd been doing this for years. As I walked to the car she trilled happily, winding her toenails into the weave of my clothes to get a better grip. She shifted politely as I seatbelted myself in. I had to remind myself that all this was new to her—she seemed like a pro.

The sound of the engine was a different matter. As it turned over, she squawked in a minor panic and flew around my head. I waited for her to realise she wasn't in immediate danger, and carefully pulled out, driving as smoothly as I could. She settled down and alighted first on my head and then on the dashboard, peering forwards and trilling with a slightly cautious curiosity.

We arrived at work five minutes early, perfect for a cigarette in the carpark before I went in. It was a good thing I was employed on a reasonable salary—I'd never be able to afford this addiction otherwise! The little pterosaur was quite judgemental, taking to the air and hovering upwind of me. Just like my judgemental brother, who also used to smoke. I smiled, knowing next time I visited him I'd be introducing him to his first ever real-life dinosaur.

I don't make the big bikkies for hanging out smoking in carparks, though. Sooner or later I had to go inside. As I had that thought and put out the cigarette, the pterosaur alighted on the back of my head and grabbed some of my hair with her wing-claws and foot-claws. She was pretending to be a hairclip! And her shiny chocolate skin would have looked quite ornamental, like polished tortoiseshell.

Eliza, my stuffy boss, was already there. "Good morning. Late again?"

I was never late. As always, I was crack on time. "Sorry, Eliza." I slid into my desk and powered up the computer, opening the folder of actionable files. I spent the next while absorbed in my work, processing quite a lot of files and setting up two zooms for late in the afternoon. One thing Eliza would never be able to fire me for was my work. She hated my guts and was just looking for an excuse, but I processed more than anybody else, and with fewer errors. I didn't like the work, but I really liked the money.

Shane came in, Eliza's Golden Boy. He had the same job I did, but because she valued him and didn't value me, I had to treat him as if he was also my boss. I gritted my teeth as I looked up and smiled at him. He was going to start the day with his usual racist shit again, as he always did. But I had to pretend to tolerate it. I desperately needed the job. He smiled back at me, like an upside-down shark.

"How's my favourite little black bitch, today?"

I couldn't punch him. I needed the money, and I didn't need the conviction for assault. I also didn't need to confirm stereotypes about my people and violence.

"Fine." I could feel the pterosaur, still pretending to be a hairclip, tighten up. No, I thought at her, you can't take out one of his eyeballs. Please don't. Please.

He sat down and played on his phone as I processed another two files. Then he fired up his own computer. I went to the ladies. When the pterosaur realised what I was doing, she flew around my head. My phone pinged. I washed my hands. A texted summons to Eliza's office. The pterosaur lodged herself on my jacket, looking for the world like a shiny, ornate steampunk brooch, every scale individually visible.

I knocked.

"Shut the door. Sit down." Her voice was irritated. "Why did you just leave the workplace?"

"I had a full bladder."

"You should have waited till the break."

"If I'd waited until the break, I would have had to urinate in my chair. And because they are cheap fabric and not leather, we would never get rid of either the moisture or the smell."

"Nevertheless." She stood up and turned her back as she rummaged through a file drawer in the bank of drawers behind her. The pterosaur saw an opportunity and took flight, landing on the edge of her cup of coffee. Holding on with all four limbs, she pissed copiously into Eliza's coffee. The acrid smell was eye-watering. By the time Eliza turned back, she was looking like a brooch again, but slightly higher on my lapel.

Eliza slapped the standard warning form on her deck. Her eyes narrowed. "Wasn't that pterodactyl's head facing the other way?"

I tried not to look guilty. "It's a pterosaur, not a pterodactyl. You can tell by … oh, never mind. It's flexible. I bent it."

"I've never seen you wear it before." It sounded like an accusation.

"Not at work, no. It's pretty versatile. I can wear it on my clothes, or as a hairclip. I might even dangle it from an ear sometimes."

"Hmmm." She was still suspicious. She picked up her cup, then recoiled. "Did you just piss yourself to prove a point?"

I was indignant. "Gosh, no! I like these clothes! That's exactly why I went to the toilet!"

She put down her cup and bent over the form, filling in the date and time, the official code for my desk's location, and checking "absent from duty" and "insubordination" from the list of suggested offences. "This is your second warning. Sign here, please."

I signed, and returned to my desk, pretending not to notice Shane smirking at me. I know he wanted me fired, but he hadn't thought it through. If I got fired, he'd have to pick up the slack, and learn how to do a decent day's work. He'd never cope. I fumed and sat down with what I hoped was an expressionless face. I pointedly started hammering away on my keyboard as he played Tetris on his phone. The pterosaur continued being the model brooch, pretty and not too conspicuous.

A moment later there was a choking sound and a scream. I looked around. The glass wall of Eliza's office had been sprayed with dinosaur-urine-flavoured coffee. More of it was dribbling from her chin. Her face was a study. I continued working expressionlessly.

The pterosaur could stay. I could use a decent friend who ate small vermin and pissed in the drinks of large vermin. From now on life was going to be a little more entertaining.

EATER OF HEARTS

I am an eater of hearts. Tender hearts.

I climb ceaselessly. I walk ceaselessly. I look into the heart of the abyss on a daily basis. Often it is a soul-clenching black. Sometimes it is a more dangerous red, seething balefully as it looks right back at me.

I walk alone through life. None can pace me. None can match me. None can love me.

Sometimes I throw many hearts into a great cauldron, and leave them overnight. They cannot escape. This is the end for them, but just the beginning for me.

When I'm not hiking, mountain-climbing or taking an interest in vulcanology, I like barbeques. I take square-cut capsicums and onions, and tender chicken hearts marinated overnight in lemon juice and exquisite spices, thread them onto wet bamboo skewers, and suspend them over smouldering coals.

I am an eater of hearts. Tender hearts.